Swimming Toward the Light

ARAB AMERICAN WRITING

Other titles in Arab American Writing

The Cairo House: A Novel
Samia Serageldin

A Community of Many Worlds: Arab Americans in New York City
Museum of the City of New York

Hayati, My Life: A Novel
miriam cooke

Letters from Cairo
Pauline Kaldas

Post Gibran: Anthology of New Arab American Writing
Munir Akash and Khaled Mattawa, eds.

The Situe Stories
Frances Khirallah Noble

Swimming Toward the Light

A NOVEL

. . .

Angela Tehaan Leone

SYRACUSE UNIVERSITY PRESS

First Edition 2007

07   08   09   10   11   12   6   5   4   3   2   1

The paper used in this publication meets the minimum requirements of
American National Standard for Information Sciences—Permanence of
Paper for Printed Library Materials, ANSI Z39.48–1984.∞™

For a listing of books published and distributed by Syracuse University Press,
visit our Web site at SyracuseUniversityPress.syr.edu.

LIBRARY OF CONGRESS CATALOGING-IN-PUBLICATION DATA

Leone, Angela Tehaan.

Swimming toward the light : a novel / Angela Tehaan Leone.—1st ed.

p. cm.—(Arab American writing)

ISBN-13: 978–0–8156–0857–8 (cloth : alk. paper)

ISBN-10: 0–8156–0857–8 (cloth : alk. paper)

1. Arab American families—Fiction. 2. Arab Americans—Fiction. I. Title.

PS3612.E577S85   2007

813'.6—dc22   2006033687

Manufactured in the United States of America

In memory of
Helena Kiatta Amouri
and Helen Amouri,
my grandmother and my aunt

. . . if my mother loved me instinctively, despite herself,

then what virtue is there in this love?

And is she thus superior to the cat who, at times,

loves her kittens, but, at other times, devours them?

—ELIZABETH WARNOCK FERNEA,
"Memoirs of a Female Physician,"
in *Women in the Middle East*

Angela Tehaan Leone is second-generation Lebanese American. Her grandparents emigrated in the 1920s to Washington, D.C., where her paternal grandfather opened what was to become Tehaan's Restaurant, well-known among Georgetown University students and Georgetown residents for over fifty years. Mrs. Leone was an adjunct professor of composition for Syracuse University and a teacher of high school English and theater arts. Her essays, poetry, and short stories have appeared in the *New York Times,* the *Washington Post,* the *Washingtonian, Ladies' Home Journal,* and numerous literary and medical journals. Her work was excerpted and discussed in Rebecca McLanahan's *Write Your Heart Out.* This is her first published novel.

Acknowledgments

I owe enormous thanks to Pat Carr, for her encouragement and suggestions; to Joanne Glenn, for responding as the novel took form; to Madge, who understands; to my husband Ray, who proofread tirelessly; to the staff of Syracuse University Press, especially Mary Selden Evans, whose faith in the novel kept me going, and to the International Women's Writing Guild, for encouraging me as a writer and as a woman.

Swimming Toward the Light

... *1* ...

Irene was seven years old when our mother first slapped her across the face, slapping so hard that one of Irene's braids whipped around and grazed our mother's cheek. There'd been other slaps, of course, and washing out Irene's mouth with soap and pulling her by the ear. But never a slap across the face. Never until that February day when snow fell in thick, fat flakes, smothering both air and ground.

From outside came the happy squeals of the neighbor children sledding on the hill. Athletic, robust boys and the girls so unafraid. My sister had only said that "No," she didn't want to take her sled and join the neighborhood children playing in the snow, and as Mama descended the stairs afterwards, she had muttered, "Dat one! Dat one should never have been born."

One morning in March, Irene sat on the edge of her bed wearing a plaid flannel robe of Dad's, its worn sleeves rolled back over her chicken-bone wrists. In the backyard, daffodil pips pushed their noses into the frigid morning air. Irene picked up a pencil she'd taken from the rusted coffee can Mama used for kitchen odds and ends. On paper from her school notebook, Irene drew one stem, then another. She leaned forward to peer outside her window. She placed pencil on paper again. She smiled. She drew. She hummed—until Mama's voice called from the bottom of the stairs, and Irene flicked her eyes toward the clock on her dresser and saw that it read twenty past eight.

Irene jumped up, yanked off her robe, reached for a blouse, buttoned it wrong, tore off the blouse, ripped a button in the process, and tossed the blouse onto the floor. She yanked a dress from its hanger, pulled it over her head, grabbed the blouse with the ripped button, stuffed it under her pillow, and shoved her feet into a pair of shoes. At 8:28, she pulled open her bedroom door to face Mama, who'd stopped on the first landing to catch her breath.

With shoulders hunched around the stalk of her body, Irene's fingers gripped the railing until her knuckles became strawberries against the whiteness of her skin. She slid one foot across a stair, down one more stair then across another. With each step she took forward, Mama backed one step down.

At the bottom of the stairs, Mama reached out to grab Irene's chin. Her forefinger pressed into a smudged pencil mark on the side of Irene's mouth. "Dirty!"

"Yes, Mama."

Mama yanked Irene's arm and shoved her toward the kitchen. "Hurry! Wash hand. Wash nail."

"Yes, Mama."

As Irene shuffled through the kitchen doorway with head down and shoulders rounding forward, Mama yelled, "Wit hot water!"

My sister was eleven years old when I first heard the full beauty of her singing voice. I'd heard her humming before as she hung out the laundry or when she was alone in the bathroom or in her room, but never had I heard the full beauty of her voice until that summer night, when Mama had gone out for an evening with the cousins.

I'd come home from work, fixed myself a plate of grape leaves with olive oil and parsley and chopped onion—a slice of bread, a wedge of cheese, and sank into a kitchen chair, which I'd positioned in line with the breeze that streamed in from the back porch. First the sound of Dad's wooden flute, his *minjareh,* then Irene's voice floated toward me.

That was the first time I heard my sister sing because singing was not allowed in our house. No raised voices of any kind. *Ssh!* Parlor windows closed. *Ssh!* No sound that might bother the neighbors. Nothing to raise eyebrows. Nothing to disturb. Only Dad playing his flute was allowed. Because he was Dad. Because Mama said so. Because.

On the back porch, Dad sat in his rocking chair with the wooden flute, handmade in Syria many years before, raised to his lips. He took in a breath, bent forward to breathe into the mouthpiece then slid his slender, ropelike fingers across the holes in the wood, floating sounds into the air.

Every evening, after dinner, he would lift the *minjareh* from its drawer in the dining room buffet and, if the air was warm enough, would slip onto the back porch and play—sometimes Arabic songs and sometimes, I believe, melodies created out of his own loneliness and need.

That night, Irene sat at his feet, more like his granddaughter than his child. Irene's legs were drawn up beside her, her fingers resting on her ankle, her eyes closed, dark hair cloaking her shoulders as she tilted her head to drink in the music's sound.

The first tune Dad played was a lonely melody. Irene hummed then wound a wordless "ooo" around the notes of the song. Then Dad played an old Arabic melody, syncopated in its rhythm, intricate in its dips and turns, while Irene hummed. After Dad had stopped playing, he laid the flute across his lap and lit a cigarette. Then the rich, silvery sound of Irene's soprano blossomed unaccompanied into song. I don't remember what she sang. Whatever it was, Irene's voice glowed as if it were stained glass replicating sound.

When Dad began to play again, his flute and Irene's voice blended, separated, and joined. He began another song, something jiglike, and Irene laughed as she made up the words—nonsense phrases like "lumidi, lumida," and "bumidi, bumida." The tune rose and picked up speed. Irene sang and made up syllables, her voice instinctively following the tune's bends and turns.

An hour into that impromptu concert, the guttural chatter of female Arabic voices sputtered at the front door. Mama was being delivered home by her cousins.

From my chair in the kitchen, I looked down the hallway to watch our mother step into the house, the silhouette of her short, round body lit by a streetlight. Without taking off her hat, she crossed to the bottom of the stairs and looked up toward the second floor for Irene. With her head tilted upward, Mama resembled a turtle—large and round in the middle with a locust leaf for its head.

Mama took the pins out of her hat, hung it on a hat-stand hook, walked into the kitchen, and headed straight toward the back porch door. I wanted to raise my hand like a traffic policeman to say, "No! Wait! Listen to your daughter sing!" But the back porch door had already crashed with an ear-shattering slam.

My sister's eyes turned toward Dad as if to say, "Talk to her for me! Tell her you want me to stay," but Dad's eyes became two dark oceans on the bony planes of his face. With a flick of her wrist, Mama motioned to Irene. "Is late! Long ago time for bed!" Then she stepped forward and scooted Irene in front of her toward the stairs as if my sister were a chicken being shooed into a pen.

Starting at the age of five, Irene had grown taller and taller. After the kitchen and bathrooms were scrubbed, Mama would pull out her crochet hook and thread to create edgings that were added to the bottom of out-worn clothes of mine. Brown trim on blue wool already edged with red. Navy attached to yellow daisies against a turquoise sea or yellow rickrack tacked to purple corduroy or a gathered pink band added to a row of crochet. Blue gingham on green. White on red-and-blue check.

By the time she started school, Irene had grown taller and thinner each year. The coffee-colored birthmark that splashed along the side of her neck seemed to enlarge with every inch my sister grew. Encouraged by Irene's height, her bony legs and arms, and the patchwork hems that barely covered her knees, neighborhood children taunted, "Scare-crow! Scare-crow!" Mama, of course, was blind to the Raggedy Ann caricature her daughter had become.

.   .   .

Through sixth grade, Mama walked Irene to school everyday, an old sweater of Dad's buttoned over the housedress that covered her Humpty-Dumpty form, one of its pockets bulging, as always, with paper napkins. When the crossing guard yelled that *she* was there to guide the students safely across the street, Mama would raise her chin in defiance, tighten her grasp of Irene's hand, and charge forward, barely missing cars that were about to make a turn.

At lunchtime Mama reappeared to hand Irene a brown grease-stained bag containing meatloaf inside Syrian bread or stuffed squash in a container of yogurt sauce.

They'd skipped Irene one grade, and when she entered the seventh grade she sat between one girl with scarlet fingernails and another who, in spite of her demure Peter Pan collar and pleated skirt, pushed out her chest to display her blooming breasts. What could Irene say to these girls about the hours she passed at home in silence? Or about how she felt she would explode with things she wanted to say and couldn't because Mama's English vocabulary consisted of only a few hundred words and because Mama had made it clear she wouldn't be interested anyway.

My sister could say nothing to her classmates about why, at recess time, she sat under the locust tree and buried herself in *Anne of Green Gables* or why she tugged at the stand-up collars of her blouses to hide the birthmark on her neck or why she averted her eyes from her "Amulcan" classmates, the word Mama used when talking about lighter-skinned citizens of the United States. Nor could Irene tell them why she ate parsley-studded meatloaf tucked into pockets of heavy homemade Arabic bread while they ate baloney and peanut butter on Wonder Bread or rye. Most probably, they would have laughed at the intensity of her shame.

After she'd entered puberty and a few girls talked brazenly about "the curse" or about how "the visitor" had arrived, my sister turned away shame-faced because Mama said "it" must never be talked about.

One afternoon, I came across my sister squatting at the side of the house, cradling a stray kitten she'd managed to coax into her arms. When she said, "Please don't tell Mama!" I remembered that for all of us, pets and dolls and stuffed animals had been forbidden in the house. "Trash" Mama called them. She'd even forced me to throw out a teddy bear that had been given to me. In time, I made my peace with this and found consolation in the dolls and pets I played with and cuddled in the houses of my friends. But Irene?

Sometimes after a school trip to the zoo, Irene would knock on my door at night. "Lottie, a monkey tried to talk to me!" or "Today, I saw a mother tiger washing her baby's face!" or "Why don't they ever let the animals come out of the cage?"

Later I found pencil drawings my sister had done—pages of squirrels and birds along with an attempt at the likeness of almost every animal in the zoo. In every drawing, finished or not, in front of the animals she'd drawn a relentless series of formidable black bars.

When Irene was fourteen years old, she was assigned to the Frank C. Tivoli High School, a two-block walk over to 35th Street, then eight blocks up to the intersection of P.

During the first week of school that year, Mama phoned me at work four times. "Irene cry. She hide and say she not go! What I do wit dat girl?" On the second day, an attendance officer escorted my sister to school—and on the next day and the next. On the first day of her second week, in music class, Toby Yanchus, two years older than the rest of the ninth graders, crawled under a row of seats and cut off two sections of rickrack and ruffles from the back of Irene's dress.

Irene's row had been standing to sing "America the Beautiful," and when they sat down, snickering rippled through the room. The teacher had insisted Irene's row stand and sing the song again, "Irene, you must project your voice and let the others partake of its beautiful sound!"

By the time Irene sat down again, when Miss McKinley turned her back to erase the board, Toby Yanchus held up the pink-and-purple row of mismatched fabric, waving it like a flag. When the bell rang, Irene reached down to touch her legs, now bare in the back above the knees. She looked once more at the trophy Toby waved in the air, stared at the whistling, laughing classmates who clustered around him, raked her nails along the inside of her arm, wrapped her arms around her stomach, and vomited on the floor.

After the principal phoned Dad at the store, Dad must have dropped everything and then caught a streetcar up Wisconsin Avenue because within forty-five minutes, Dad walked into the principal's office.

Head bowed, as if he were expecting some kind of punishment, Dad stood in front of the principal's massive oak desk, a poster-sized framed photograph of President Eisenhower, and a wall-mounted American flag. Dad's stained white apron was visible under his gray jacket while his nicotine-stained fingers danced along the wide brim of the hat he held in his hand.

Irene sat with her eyes focused on the floor as the principal explained what had happened and told them that Toby Yanchus would be removed from all of Irene's classes. "We'll certainly do our best to see that nothing like this ever happens again," the principal said.

Dad nodded. "Tank you." Then he reached for Irene's hand and pulled her to her feet. He slapped his hat on his head, ran his fingers from back to front along the center crease of the hat, said "Tank you" again, then walked his daughter through the hall and out onto the sidewalk.

At the corner, Dad looked both ways for cars, then took Irene's hand and led the way across the street. It was probably the first time any of us had walked with our father hand-in-hand.

Ten minutes after they arrived at the house, Irene, dressed in a tartan jumper and a clean white blouse, stepped out onto the porch where Dad sat in his rocker smoking a cigarette. Coffee in two cups with saucers had been placed upon the floor along with a hard roll on a paper napkin. Dad reached for one cup and saucer and brought it to his lap. He nodded toward the other cup then to Irene. "For you, Ah-weh, coffee, warm."

Irene sat down, reached for the cup, and drank. Dad picked up the roll, snapped it in half, and placed half on Irene's lap. "*Hoobez*. Good for when you sick." He picked up his cup and saucer, rocked back in the chair, dipped the end of his roll into his coffee, then sucked the wet end.

Late September sun beamed through the slats of the grape arbor that stood to the side of Mama's back porch. When their cups were empty and the roll was gone, Dad pushed himself out of the cane seat of his rocking chair, then walked over to stand behind Irene. Did he think about resting his hand on her shoulder? It's important to me to believe that he would have if in our family that kind of thing were done.

Then Dad opened the screen door to the kitchen, and, while my sister sat alone in the sun, he picked up his hat from the kitchen table, slipped on his jacket, and disappeared into the shadows of the front hall to finish the long hours of his day.

. . . *2* . . .

The Yanchus family lived one block down from Mama in one of the row houses we used to call shacks. On school mornings, nine sleepy children, four boys and five girls, tumbled out of the doorway, squabbling over notebooks, pencils, and vanilla wafer cookies from a box. As noisy and rumpled as they were, they seemed golden to me, light-haired and fair-skinned, laughing and chattering in ways we'd been told were far too loud.

Their mother, Eloise Yanchus, was a plain-looking woman of medium height who shopped at the D.G.S. with her apron still tied around her waist. Her pink-cheeked face smiled easily. She was easy to talk to even when there wasn't much to say.

Rumors were that Mr. Yanchus drank so much they fired him from his job as a streetcar conductor and that one night, when Ralph Alan was eleven years old, he had knocked his father out cold in order to stop the beating Mr. Yanchus was giving his wife and one of the younger girls.

Several months later, an ambulance had arrived at the Yanchus house and had taken Mr. Yanchus away. Within months, the father, a wiry, red-faced man, reappeared on the porch in a wheelchair. The neighborhood gossip said that the empty balloons of Mr. Yanchus's trousers concealed the fact that no legs existed below either of his knees—sugar diabetes, the neighbors said.

Ralph Alan was close to six feet in height, but the extra padding of his body made him look chunky rather than tall. His red-cheeked coloring matched his mother's, and his wheat-colored hair was shorn in a crew-cut. Ralph Alan rarely accompanied his siblings when they tumbled out of the house headed for school. "Simple," they said about him. Mama crossed herself whenever she passed him on the street.

From early March to late November, Ralph Alan Yanchus could be recognized by his blue-and-red-checked shirt and brown corduroy trousers. He spent his day going back and forth to the store for milk and bread for his mother and cigarettes and beer for his father.

Ralph Alan swept and scrubbed the Yanchus front porch. I even saw him hanging out the wash. When I passed him as he swept the porch, his back bent, his eyes straining toward a leaf or twig or beetle shell, he'd look up from whatever he was doing, and his eyebrows would rise in anticipation. A grin would spill onto his face as he said, "Hi ya, Lottie!"

In good weather, Ralph Alan would position his father's wheelchair on the front porch in a sun-lit place and sit near him on a step. They'd stay there, Mr. Yanchus smoking cigarette after cigarette with Ralph Alan looking toward his father with a smile on his face. Weather permitting, at least once a week Ralph Alan wheeled Mr. Yanchus to Sugar's Drugstore for ice cream and sometimes even to Weismuller's to buy a sandwich and a Coke. It seemed impossible that trouble between them, if there had been any, could ever have occurred.

Toby, the second-oldest Yanchus, was the troublemaker who'd cut off the bottom of Irene's dress. I never would've known about the incident except that one day I answered the insistent ringing of Mama's front doorbell, and from behind the screen door, I saw a reed-thin but tough-looking kid whom I vaguely recognized as the second oldest Yanchus boy from down the street. One of his hands was jammed into the back pocket of his denim jeans. The other hand clutched folded material that looked like it had once been part of a dress.

Toby Yanchus eyed me warily. Whereas Ralph Alan's hair was the color of summer wheat, Toby's slicked-back hair was the color of wet sand. I expected to see a pack of cigarettes stuck in the rolled up sleeve of his white T-shirt but there was none. He lifted up the fabric and held it in front of him as if it were laden with germs.

I spoke from behind the screen door. "Yes?"

"You're not Mrs. Awtooah." His voice was deeper than I would've expected.

"And you're not the newspaper boy."

He shrugged and gave me a half-hearted grin. He flapped the fabric toward the screen. "Ma sent me over to give you this."

I pushed open the screen door and took hold of the fabric. "Well, at least you're honest about it. And you did return a part of the dress."

He eyed me before raising an eyebrow in acknowledgment of my half-hearted compliment. He shoved his hands into his pockets, pulled them out, put them behind his back, then shoved them into his pockets again. "Ma might call just to see how I did."

I nodded and stepped back inside. I closed the screen door, slipped the hook into the catch, and, remembering the guilt of my own teen-aged transgressions, said, "Don't worry. I'll tell her you did fine."

The Courtyard Apartments on Prospect Street consisted of four-story-high apartments made from an old Georgian mansion that was one of the oldest houses in Georgetown. The house and now the apartments were built around a courtyard where ancient plantings of overgrown wisteria, dogwood, boxwood, and azaleas spilled onto each other in the corners of its shaded yard. Stone benches dotted the cement path that meandered like an English garden through the courtyard's center. A tunnel-like stucco corridor linked the courtyard with the street.

The courtyard was a quiet place. Apartment windows rarely opened onto the yard itself, and family squabbles were never aired. Wrens and finches and blue jays fluttered and squabbled after juniper berries while squirrels ferreted out hickory nuts, swishing their tails as they hustled away. The courtyard was a place of cool breezes in summer and of protection from March winds and thick, wet December snow.

As teenagers, we often "made out" in the corners of the courtyard because it was quiet and hidden from view. Irene told me that she often took paper and a pencil into the courtyard, tucked herself into a corner near the back wall and sketched the squirrels that crossed her path. By the time she was fourteen, stopping off at the courtyard became a regular part of Irene's return home after school.

On one unusually warm Friday near the middle of October, she had just edged through the arches of the tunnel entrance into the courtyard when her eye caught the red and blue of a shirt and brown corduroy trousers. Ralph Alan, the oldest Yanchus boy, lay on his stomach with his coat spread under him. With his finger, he seemed to be following the movements of a winding procession of ants.

"Come over here and see," he said to Irene without turning his head in her direction. With his eyes fixed on the ground in front of him, he beckoned her over. "Did you know that ants can remember things, and they can even fix their mistakes? Come over here and watch. They leave messages for each other about changing direction so none of them can get lost. Right now, God's helping them find a place to eat."

Irene took one step forward. "You're Toby's brother, aren't you?"

Without turning his head toward her, Ralph Alan nodded. "But I'm not Toby." He waved her over. "Come over here and see the parade. Some ants are fighters, and the winners even take slaves."

Irene inched one foot forward, then another. Remaining a safe distance from where Ralph Alan lay, she sat down on the edge of a stone bench and tried to peer over Ralph Alan's shoulder to see what he was doing. When she coughed, Ralph Alan flapped his hand motioning her to be still.

Fifteen minutes later Ralph Alan rolled over, slipped his hands behind his head, looked up at the sky, and smiled. He lay there for a minute, then pushed himself up and folded his legs Indian style. He looked straight at Irene as if he'd known her all his life and said, "Gosh, that sure was fun!"

His eyes focused on Irene's face, on the thick wavy mass of her hair, then moved to her neck and settled on her birthmark, which no one except Mama had ever touched. With one fluid movement, Ralph Alan shifted forward to his knees. Before she saw what he was doing, he'd raised his arm and leaned in toward Irene's neck until the pink pads of his fingertips rested on her skin.

Irene's body stiffened, but she didn't pull away. His fingers touched lightly, then traced the ragged map of her birthmark's edges and lingered for a moment on the place where they'd begun. When he pulled his hand away, he nodded solemnly like a doctor who is satisfied that his treatment is going to work.

He wiped his palms on the front of his shirt then extended his hand. "Hi. You're Irene. I'm Ralph Alan. I sure am glad you're here!"

She hesitated for an instant then raised her hand to meet Ralph Alan's, and for the first time in a long time, spontaneously, she smiled.

After her first meeting with Ralph Alan, Irene spent evenings in her room calculating how soon would be too soon to visit the Courtyard Apartments again. She spent more time than she had in her entire life staring at herself in the mirror, her finger tracing over and over again the outline of her birthmark.

"I'm ugly, aren't I, Mama?" she said as she set the dinner table one evening.

Mama stopped squeezing lemon on the chicken and turned to look at her youngest daughter. "Ugly? What ugly? Allah make everyone little bit different is all." She nodded as if pleased with what she'd thought to say. She turned back to the baking pan. "Little bit different fine. Little bit different good."

Two weeks after the meeting in the courtyard, Irene pulled out sweaters, blouses, skirts, and dresses and tried them on. On the nights I was at home, Irene would walk across the hall and ask me how I thought she looked—an unusual question for my sister at that time but I was too preoccupied with my own life to give it much thought.

After discarding two sweaters and a blue corduroy dress, Irene chose a maroon corduroy skirt and a blouse whose neck only partly covered her birthmark. She tried them on and stepped forward toward the mirror, then made a halfway turn around. She slipped out of the blouse and her cotton bra. She ran her fingers over her neck, down the side of her chest then up again, this time inching closer toward the two brown circles that stood out from the two plums that were her breasts.

"Nipples" she'd heard the girls call them in school. "Nipples." The word sounded like dirty toys, something that a mother would grab away from a baby, like the pebbles Mama used to tell her she mustn't pick up in the backyard, like something too unimportant to look at more than once.

The next morning, she did not ask Mama to put her hair in braids. She brushed and brushed the thick coils of her hair. Then she stepped back to inspect the stiff wavy triangle that had its base at her shoulders. If she had looked carefully, she might have seen that, with the high cheekbones of her face, she almost looked like an Egyptian princess, except that her nose was too sharp near its end, her face too long, her forehead too high. She searched her drawer and pulled out the green velvet headband Mama allowed her to wear for special occasions.

In school that day, more than one teacher said, "Irene Awtooah, are you daydreaming again?"

When, finally, the afternoon bell rang, she slipped out faster than usual from her desk. She was faster, too, in grabbing her plaid wool coat and loose-leaf notebook from her locker.

Outside, clutching the notebook to her chest, she walked the two extra blocks, then over three more until she saw the solid brick outline of the Courtyard Apartments. She stopped before entering the narrow passageway, pulled up her gray ribbed kneesocks then walked down the brick-lined corridor.

When she stepped into the courtyard, she thought it was empty. Then she spotted a red-and-blue shirt and brown corduroy trousers. Ralph Alan lay on his back, his jacket spread under him, his hands underneath his head, his body taking up the center of the main courtyard path. He pushed himself up and sat with his long legs sprawled in front of him. The stubbles of his wheat-colored hair gleamed in the afternoon light. With two hands he pulled his long legs in toward his body, then folded them Indian style. He shifted forward to pat the ground across from him. "Come sit."

Irene did not move.

Ralph Alan patted the ground again. "Be nice to get acquainted. You and me being neighbors and all. Unless . . . unless . . . you got too many friends already? All those friends you make at school?"

"Friends?" Irene's eyes widened. "No. Not too many. Not many friends at all." She turned to rest her notebook on a nearby bench.

When she turned back, Ralph Alan was shaking out his jacket. He laid it on the brick-covered ground and indicated she should sit down where the corduroy stretched across the ground. "There. Now you don't have to worry about dirtying up." He raised his hand, palm up, toward Irene.

Irene had just stepped forward when a two-fingered whistle sliced through the air. She jerked back her hand and snapped her head toward the street.

Ralph Alan looked toward the street and shrugged. "That's only Toby letting me know Ma wants me home."

"Toby comes in here?"

"Toby can't stand the courtyard—says the walls remind him of a jail."

"Toby's been in jail?"

Ralph Alan shrugged, then waved Irene toward the space he'd made on the ground. "Come on. I got a while yet. Ma won't be missing me for a time."

Irene turned her head toward the street and listened. A blue jay flapped into the courtyard, squawked, then flew away. Irene's eyes followed its departure then turned back to Ralph Alan. "Well, okay . . . if you say so. Maybe just for a little while." She eased her fingers into his upturned palm, leaned her body toward him and lowered herself to sit on the jacket he'd spread for her upon the ground.

The third time she met with Ralph Alan, he immediately looked toward her when she entered the courtyard and smiled with his "Hi ya, Irene!" Without hesitation, my sister settled onto a bench and jammed her hands into her pocket and turned her face up toward the sun. "Say my name again, would you Ralph Alan?"

Ralph Alan smiled as if he were pleased to help her out. "Irene."

"Usually, I hate it when someone says my name. It's always Mama calling me about something I've done wrong or the teacher asking me for an answer I don't know. When I hear my name, I want to crawl under a bed and become a speck of dust—but not today. The way you say it, my name sounds . . ." she fell silent, thinking. "It sounds . . . almost nice!"

Ralph Alan leaned his head back against the tree and closed his eyes. "Well, it is nice! You're nice!" Then he bunched his lips as if he were going to whistle and let out a long slow breath on top of which floated the word, "Irene."

A plane droned overhead, then banked and turned away. In the silence that followed, Ralph Alan repeated, "Irene," then again, "Irene."

Later that day, I came home from work to find Irene dusting the front parlor. Apparently, she'd already wiped down the Nippon vase, cleaned the already-clean ashtrays, dusted the mantel, the radiator tops, underneath the couch, and the crook-necked brass floor lamp.

"What's the matter, Irene? What on earth is going on?"

Irene straightened from the andirons she was polishing, and her smile brightened into one I'll never forget. "Lottie! Lottie! I've finally found a friend!"

3

Mama was born in the area of Syria that would, in 1920, officially be re-
named Greater Lebanon. At the age of thirteen, Mama was betrothed to
Dad. Barely three months after their marriage, they traveled by steamer to
Australia to escape the rampages of the Ottoman Turks against Christians.

In Australia, Dad was given a backpack and dry goods, was taught the
words "Want any-ting, Miss-us?" and sent out into the countryside to sell.
Eventually, he owned his own horse-drawn cart and ventured into
sparsely populated areas on trips of six weeks or more.

Formally posed photographs show Dad's long, somber face and
Abraham Lincoln body towering over Mama, whose body grew wider
and more solid after the birth of each child until one photo shows a dark-
haired petite beauty transformed into Humpty-Dumpty in petticoats and
skirt.

After spending four years in Australia, the family moved to New
Zealand, where work was easier to find. Ten years after that, in 1927 when
I was an infant, the family sailed across the Pacific Ocean, then traveled by
train from California to Washington, D.C., where Mama's cousins settled
us into a life in the United States.

Elias, Mama's firstborn and only son, lived with Cousin Usma, whose
only child was also a son. My sisters Belle and Rose lived across the street
from Cousin Usma, and Mama and Dad and I settled in ten blocks away
with Soutine, the wife of one of the cousins, who had a daughter five years
older than I was. After I was weaned, I spent every afternoon with
Soutine's daughter while members of the Ladies' Club of the Syrian Ortho-

dox Church introduced Mama to the ways of her new and probably terrifying world.

Within three years, Dad borrowed money, something he'd never done before, and bought a small brick row house on Prospect Street. With help from her cousins, Mama moved into the first home of her own. Soon, the cousins and various members of the Syrian Ladies' Club visited regularly, gossiping and playing cards while I spent afternoons with Cousin Soutine's daughter either in Mama's backyard or on the daybed in the kitchen.

For the first five years, Dad worked at the fruit stand owned by a relative's husband. A few years later, he bought a small neighborhood grocery store in partnership with two other Syrian men. He worked from six in the morning until seven or eight at night. Once I saw Mama and Dad approaching the house from different directions, each with head down. When they met at the front door, a nod from one to the other was the only visible acknowledgment that the other one was there.

Mama learned enough English to speak haltingly to the butcher when she bought groceries at the D.G.S. and to say "A-low!" into the telephone receiver. For more complicated communication, she relied on her children or on Dad, whose English was halting but clear enough to get by.

Her children, of course, learned the meaning of her most important orders: *skiteh* (enough of that!), *y'allah* (get moving!), and *"la!"* (the one-syllable tongue-lashing with which Mama told us "no!" Otherwise, the language of my parents' birth became their own private language, and since my older siblings had suffered through taunts about dark skin and foreign looks, the four of us were happy to disown most aspects of our parents' past.

Among her relatives and Syrian acquaintances, Mama was seen as "the shy one" and "the sweet one" who welcomed visitors with a dimpled smile. Every other week, Mama accepted callers from the Syrian Ladies' Club of St. George's Church. Days before the visit, she and her daughters swept, dusted, and polished the front parlor to a pearly shine. The day before visiting day, if Mama discovered dust on the sideboard or a coffee stain not completely scoured from a cup, she'd come at us with both hands slapping, her words like windmill paddles in a storm.

Then, if Mama took to her bed with a headache the day before the visit, as she often did, our job was to bring her washcloths rinsed in warm water and vinegar to lay upon her head and to finish whatever scrubbing and polishing still needed to be done.

When visiting day arrived, in spite of any lingering headache pain, Mama sat demurely with her guests, her ankles crossed, smiling as she listened and nodded until she noticed an empty plate or coffee cup. Then she would flick her black button eyes to one of us or snap her fingers as a signal for us to bring more coffee, more sugar, and more pastries to satisfy her guests.

As far as I know, no one suspected that Mama could threaten her children with eyes that sliced right to your soul or that she could back one of us against a wall, unleash a torrent of Arabic, slap us across the face or pull us by the ear or—if the offense had been verbal—force open our mouths and sprinkle pepper onto our tongues and down our throats.

My older sister, Belle, told me that when Mama had caught her wearing lipstick, Mama had walked up to her and "whipped out a handkerchief so fast, it was on my mouth before I ever saw it coming. I swear that hand of hers felt like a vise clamped around my jaw!"

Elias, the firstborn and only male of Mama's children, managed to escape these tortures. From the day he was born, even after he moved hundreds of miles away, Elias stood out as being Mama's little prince who could do no wrong.

By the time Mama was forty-four, Elias, Belle, and my other sister, Rose, had moved away from home—in the case of Elias and Rose, far away from home. I was fourteen and out of the house more than I was in it. For several years before that, Mama had pretty much turned my care over to Belle and Rose.

Dad was gone from before dawn until the evening, and loneliness must have darkened many of Mama's afternoons until well into the hours of the early night. Then, when Mama was forty-four, a miracle took place and Irene was conceived.

Mama became the envy of her cousins and the entire Syrian Ladies' Club. Mama could once again bare her breast to the fragrant warmth of a hungry child.

As soon as people saw Irene's ruddy cheeks ballooning with frequent smiles, they forgot the birthmark shaped like the state of Florida that splashed along the side of her neck.

With the rest of us, there'd never been money for a carriage, but this time, Dad bought a used one, and Mama strolled up Prospect Street, stopping to tuck blankets more snugly around her child, to reposition the pillow, to rest her hand on her daughter's cheek as if to remind herself that Irene was really there. I'd tiptoe past the front bedroom when Mama rocked Irene. Mama's different, I remember thinking. My goodness, Mama's really changed!

For the first three years of her life Irene was the happiest baby I ever saw. Play "itsy-bitsy spider" with her and she giggled and chuckled, her little-girl voice sounding like carillon chimes. When you said "that's enough" and walked away, her eyebrows would rise and furrow ever so slightly—not in a pout, not starting a tantrum, simply as a plea to return and resume the fun.

And musical? On summer nights when Dad sat on the porch playing his wooden flute, I'd hold my hands around Irene's waist as her hips swayed in perfect rhythm, her head back, her dark eyes sparkling. And when the song was done, she'd clap her hands together for the music, for her audience, and for herself.

The influenza came in February soon after Irene turned three. For five days, Mama sat in darkness with her feverish child. She neither ate nor slept, refusing to let either me or even Dad touch Irene until her forehead had cooled.

Then Mama came down with the flu herself and required hours of rest. If Mama wasn't well enough to follow her toddler around the house, she forced a canvas harness over Irene's head, clipped a strap to the metal hook on the belt, tied the other end of the strap to a bedpost, and locked Irene behind the closed door of a room with juice, water, and zwieback within reach.

Even after Mama recovered, whenever she browned onions or cubed lamb, Irene was placed on the daybed in the kitchen and kept there with a barrier made of braided rope tied from the brass bar at one end to its twin bar at the other end of the bed. Whenever Mama hung out wash, Irene was harnessed and tied to a post nearest to the double clothesline in the back yard. The cousins were forbidden to visit if any of them had shown recent signs of a cold. The only time Irene was with other children was when she held tightly to Mama's hand during a walk to the drugstore or the D.G.S.

In a photograph of my sister at eight or nine years old, she sits on a pony that is being lead by a boy a few years older than she, probably a distant cousin at a family gathering at Great Falls or Hains Point. In that photograph, my sister's sparkling eyes and ready smile have vanished. In their place, I see loneliness and fear.

The November Irene met Ralph Alan, red leaves clung to maple trees and in the courtyard white chrysanthemums bloomed.

For most of the time they spent together, Ralph Alan and Irene sat in silence. "Not a silence," she told me later, "like in school when the teacher calls on you for the answer and your mind turns into mud, or like the silence at the dinner table when you feel smothered by the anger no one talks about." She said the silence with Ralph Alan was "like a walk in the country, like standing alone on a star-filled night, like the silence that must come after the crash of a wave and you see you're dry and standing on warm sand."

Even in the cool days of November, Ralph Alan wore his short-sleeved red-and-blue-checked shirt. On cold days, his brown corduroy coat was spread out on the ground like a blanket marking his place at the base of the courtyard's oldest oak tree. On rainy days, the coat became a tent over his head.

Sometimes, he'd jump up and take my sister's hand as soon as she appeared. "Look, Irene! You gotta see!" Then he'd pull her in the direction of a bird's nest he'd just discovered or a circle of mushrooms in a far, wet corner of the yard. On sunny days, they'd walk the thirty yards up the incline at the far end of the courtyard and stand in silence looking down at the Potomac River, its waters glistening silver in the light.

"Why are you so afraid, Irene?" Ralph Alan asked one day in early December.

Irene looked up at him from where she sat scratching patterns with a stick in a patch of dirt. "Me? You talking about me?"

"It's just that I used to watch you going to the store or coming home from school, and I'd say to myself 'It's not right for a girl to feel so afraid.' "

"You used to see me? You noticed me?"

"Couldn't help but listen to you sing your pretty little songs."

"My songs? You heard me singing?"

"Of course. Then I got to asking 'How come that girl who sings so pretty is looking so sad?' "

"It's just that Mama worries about me a lot. She gets mad if I'm not home when I'm supposed to be. Mama's old, you know. She had me when she was past forty years old. Having me nearly made her die."

"Well, looks to me like she got lucky having you be her daughter."

"You wouldn't be saying that just to make fun, would you?"

Ralph Alan's face darkened as he shook his head. "I told you I'm not Toby, Irene."

On a cloudy Saturday that was unusually warm for November, Irene ducked into the courtyard on her way back from borrowing a bag of rice from Cousin Usma down the street.

Ralph Alan was seated on the ground in his usual place, his legs stretched out in front of him. His shoulders hunched forward as he worked at cutting notches into a twig.

Irene took off the gloves Mama made her wear and stuffed them in her pocket. She put the bag of rice down on the end of a bench, walked over to see what Ralph Alan was doing, then walked to a pile of leaves, picked up a handful, crushed them with her fingers, and let them fall like snowflakes onto the ground.

"Ralph Alan, do you ever think God doesn't like you? Like He thinks it was a mistake you were born?"

"God doesn't think like that, Irene."

Irene bent to pick up another handful of leaves. "Mama says my birthmark's God's punishment for the pain I caused her when I was born. Mama says God sees everything, that He knows all the bad thoughts inside your head."

Ralph Alan put down the twig he was cutting then shook his head. "God doesn't punish people, Irene. He's just not that kind."

Irene opened her hand and let the leaf pieces float to the ground. She walked over to a maple tree and ran her hand along the trunk, scraping her nail against the bark. "How do you know? How do you know what God's like at all?"

Ralph Alan shrugged. "He tells me."

"But God doesn't talk to ordinary people like you and me!"

Ralph Alan pulled his legs in toward his body, Indian style. He reached out to pluck a blade of grass. "The night they took Pop to the hospital, all of us were real scared, and Ma told us if we were real still and quiet and listened, we'd hear God saying, 'Everything will be all right.' "

"And did you? Did you hear Him?"

"Two days later right here in the courtyard, I heard something kinda like whispering—almost like it was saying 'don't you worry, Ralph Alan. Everything will be all right.' "

"And was it?"

He nodded solemnly. "Doctor said it was a miracle Pop didn't die."

· "But how did you know it was God?"

Ralph Alan shrugged. "You get to know after a while."

Irene pulled her gloves from her coat pocket and put them on. "Well, I don't see how you can hear someone you can't see at all!"

"But He's here. You can hear Him if you try."

Irene turned around, looked up toward the sky, then walked toward the far wall of the courtyard where she stood for several minutes. Abruptly, she turned back to Ralph Alan. "He's right here in the courtyard?"

He nodded.

Again, Irene looked toward the sky. "All I see is clouds getting darker."

"Didn't you ever think it was God who told you to cross the street that first time you came into the courtyard?"

She shook her head. "I came here that day because I needed a place to sit—because I wasn't ready to go home."

Ralph Alan opened his mouth to respond but noisy, fat raindrops started to fall.

Irene pulled up the collar of her coat and looked toward the black clouds moving across the sky. "I'm gonna be late if I don't leave right now! Mama's probably worrying. She's probably got a headache, too!" In seven strides she was into the corridor and on her way home.

"Irene!" Ralph Alan called out when he saw that the brown bag of rice Irene had been carrying was still perched on the end of the bench. He tucked it under his coat as the raindrops turned into a downpour.

An hour later, after the storm had ended, Cousin Usma called to ask if the rice she'd given Mama had been enough. When Irene told Mama she'd left the rice in the courtyard, Mama slapped Irene, called her "Stupid! Lazy!" then ordered Irene back to the cousin's house. When Irene opened the front porch door to head down the street, there, tucked into a corner of the porch, exactly where Irene would see it, was a brown paper bag of rice that was absolutely dry.

Two weeks later, in early December, Irene left the house to buy butter and sugar at the D.G.S. When she walked into the courtyard, she found Ralph Alan on his knees in the farthest corner, his back turned to the entrance. He seemed to be staring at something on the ground in front of him. He whipped his head around and held up his hand. "Wait! Don't come any closer!"

"Can I at least walk over there?"

He studied the bench she pointed to and said, "Sure, but stay there until I say you can come."

She put down the bag, jammed her hands in her pockets, sat, and waited until Ralph Alan signaled that she could walk toward him. "It's an early Christmas present—sort of."

"But I didn't get you one."

"It doesn't matter." He dug into his pocket, pulled out a handkerchief, then bent over and dusted something on the ground. "You can come and see it now."

Irene walked to where he was kneeling, leaned closer, and squinted. "Oh! Oh! Ralph Alan!" She knelt on the ground and reached out her hand to touch what lay in front of her.

"I did it a few days ago. Five letters—see?" His fingers traced five letters inscribed in a rectangular slab of concrete that had been set into the ground. His hand moved to the right corner of the slab and the outline of a bird. "And see this, too?"

"Ralph Alan, it's beautiful!"

"We can cover it over with leaves so no one will see but you and me. You can come and look at it any time!"

When she moved her hand back to the first letter, Ralph Alan leaned forward again. Their shoulders touched under the December sun, and one soprano voice and one foggy baritone sounded out five letters of the name imbedded in the concrete slab: "I-R-E-N-E."

4

In the first week of February, Irene's singing voice was "discovered" by two ladies who lived in the neighborhood. My sister was almost fifteen years old.

I'd first met Mama's new next-door neighbor, Mary Ellen Twitchell, in the fall of that year. She was a friendly, full-bosomed woman who'd been born on a farm outside Richmond and had fallen in love with music in her earliest years.

From the first time she heard Irene humming or singing from the back porch or when she hung out the wash, Mary Ellen stopped whatever she was doing and listened. If Mary Ellen was near the window using her sewing machine, she took her foot off the pedal and stopped its whirring. If she was reading, she put down her book and slid her chair closer to the window. For almost four months, she listened. Then she called her friend Edna O'Malley.

Edna was as taut and spare as Mary Ellen was soft and large. An Ohio woman, Edna had defied her family to study singing in New York City. She had bought a one-way bus ticket to Manhattan, taken up residence in a YWCA dorm, and gotten a job as a sales girl at Macy's to pay for lessons and room and board until she married and moved to Washington, D.C. Bony and energetic, with pock-marked cheeks, Edna directed the junior choir at St. John's Church and gave piano lessons even though arthritis had slowed the movement of her fingers over the keys. Her Saturdays were spent listening to the Metropolitan Opera broadcasts from New York.

"Amazing!" Edna said to Mary Ellen the first time she heard Irene sing. Four times she came over to Mary Ellen's to listen when Irene was singing on the porch or in the backyard.

One frigid winter afternoon, the two women, bundled in winter coats, rang Mama's doorbell. As the ice of February air streamed into the front hall, Mary Ellen, the next-door neighbor whom Mama had never said two words to, began to talk. "We felt we needed to—"

"—to say something about the extraordinary talent your daughter has," the thinner women interrupted.

Stone-faced, Mama listened.

"Don't worry, Mrs. Awtooah! It's nothing bad." Mary Ellen assured Mama.

"And we're certain that once we tell you about the extraordinary potential of your daughter's singing voice, you'll want to cooperate as completely as you can," added Mrs. O'Malley.

"We know it must be difficult for you to understand things in a country so different from yours, but we want to help Irene—it's really that simple." Mary Ellen stepped toward Mama. "My goodness, we're causing you to freeze—us standing here blabbing. Here, let me give you my number so we can talk at a better time." Mary Ellen pulled out paper and pencil and began to write.

Mama took the paper then dropped her head in a nod.

"Please do call us soon," Edna added.

Two hours later, Mama called me at work to try to explain what had happened. Later, I looked over the paper Mary Ellen had given Mama. It gave a phone number and said, "Please call." The next day, I phoned and set a time for Mama and me to visit, which turned out to be the very next afternoon.

"Your daughter's gifted," Mary Ellen said, after she introduced Edna and walked us into her living room.

"I'm sure, Mrs. Awtooah, that you can see the imperative nature of helping your daughter develop her extraordinary voice." Edna said from a straight-backed chair near the piano.

Mary Ellen smiled. "Lessons are actually what we had in mind, piano first and a little bit of music theory. We can start at my house—right here, right next door."

"Of course, she must learn the basics of piano first," Edna interrupted. "Mary Ellen can do that, but we also want to mold that marvelous vocal gift she has and especially to teach her voice placement so that she won't misuse her voice—that's where I hope to help. A singing voice is such a fragile instrument, you know."

Although I couldn't entirely understand, I began to see that my sister's singing voice was a part of her physical being, something like a runner's naturally muscular legs.

"You have to talk to Irene as soon as possible and see what she thinks about this idea," Edna continued. "We want her to know we won't take away from her school studies—"

Mary Ellen interrupted, "—or from helping you around the house, Mrs. Awtooah. As a matter of fact, I was just telling Edna how often I've noticed Irene shaking out mops, sweeping the porch, and hanging out wash. My goodness, what a helpful child! So, if everybody agrees, I want her to come next door for some piano basics with me and then have Edna start working with her as soon after that as we can."

Throughout the conversation, Mama held her mouth in a tight, thin line. With each comment from one of the ladies, Mama nodded like a duck dipping its head into a pond to spear a minnow. We left with a promise from Mary Ellen that she'd let us know when we might bring Irene over so that all of us could talk about the possibility of lessons starting soon.

"What dey want from us?" Mama said that evening at dinner. "Want someting for sure!" She ladled more spinach and lentil soup into Dad's plate, but her words were directed toward me. "Tink we have money for lessons? Tink girl who cannot be school on time learn play and sing?" Dad continued folding his Syrian bread, then mopping up the brown liquid from his bowl. Irene might as well not have been in the room.

Mama went on and on about the "Amulcan" women who'd come knocking on her front door. Like the rest of the members of St. George's Syrian Ladies' Club, Mama minimized contact with any light-skinned "outsiders," whom she derisively referred to as "Amulcan"—a practice, I've come to believe, that consoled them about being outsiders in a country so different from the one they used to call home.

That night, after Dad had finished eating and pushed back his chair to light a match on the sole of his shoe, I tried to explain to him what had happened that afternoon. He smoked and nodded. I told him the two women were honestly excited about Irene's voice and seemed to be sincere. He continued to smoke and nod, looking at the empty dishes on the table rather than at me.

Irene picked at her food and looked down at her plate. We all knew that our brother, Elias, had been given two years of violin lessons when he was twelve years old but that when our sister Rose had asked for piano lessons, Mama had said, "Lesson?" then laughed, never even bothering to say "no." For a son, they would scrape together the money. A daughter was an entirely different thing.

Dad slurped his coffee from his saucer, occasionally nodding as if he were agreeing with a customer who'd said "Wasn't today a pleasant day?" I was used to his indifference about what had clearly been defined as "a woman's world," but this was one of those times when I wanted to shake him and yell, "Say something, won't you? Speak up for your daughter for once! Can't you manage that at all?"

Instead, I took my plate to the sink and picked up a dish towel. A few minutes later, when Dad moved his dessert plate to the side, I turned back. "So, what do you think about Irene taking singing lessons from the lady next door and her friend? They certainly seem nice, and the chance would be something special for Irene." Dad nodded, pushed back his chair and stood, turned toward the buffet, which housed his *minjareh,* pulled out his flute, then walked back through the kitchen in front of me and out through the back porch door.

.   .   .

Three days later, after I came home late from work, Irene opened her bedroom door as soon as she heard me reach the top of the stairs. "Lottie? Can
you tell me what Mama's talking about? About Mary Ellen from next door
and a friend of hers? About you and Mama going to their house? Something about me and my singing?"

"You mean Mama hasn't told you?" When Irene shook her head, I
stepped into her room and closed the door. "It's you—this is all about you
and that beautiful voice of yours—that gift you've been given by God!"

Irene turned her head and looked away. "But why did they pick me
out? In school the music teacher says my voice is something special, but
other people in class have special voices, too."

"Not special like your voice, Irene. Believe me, not special like yours."
I stepped back and looked at her. I squinted, then looked again. My sister
was three inches taller than I was. She was tall, but not outrageously tall for
a young woman. Her face, which was too long, had Mama's creamy com-
plexion, and when it filled out as she got older, with those wide brown velvet eyes, she'd be a knockout on the stage.

I closed one eye like a painter sizing up his subject. "I can see you on
stage in a slender off-white satin dress with your dark hair pulled back and
rhinestone earrings . . ." I stepped closer and reached out a finger toward
her face, "With eyeliner and rouge, and just imagine an orchestra behind
you! And spotlights! All because of Irene Awtooah's very special voice!"

Irene pulled away and walked toward her bureau mirror. She touched
her face with her fingers, and, like a blind person "seeing," traced the
lines of her high cheekbones, the slight indentation of her chin and
down the long, lean lines of her neck where her fingers rested briefly on her
birthmark.

She had no idea how attractive she could be when her face filled out
and a hairdresser did something with her mop of unruly hair.

"You say they've asked Mama to do what?"

"They've asked her to let them give you lessons. Mary Ellen will teach
you about the piano first, and then when school lets out, her friend, Edna,

will start working with your voice. Edna studied singing many years ago in New York."

"In New York? You mean where the Saturday opera on the radio comes from? The one we have to listen to and write about in music class at school?"

I nodded. "Mary Ellen's heard bits and pieces of your singing when you're out in the yard or on the porch. She was so impressed, she told her friend to come over to hear you—and finally they knocked on Mama's door."

"Impressed with me?" Irene turned back to face the mirror, looking at her reflection, her head tilted slightly to the side, her eyes squinting, as if she were studying an alien face.

"Mama needs time to think about it—and, of course, they want to talk to you. They are going to talk to you, and whether you go ahead with lessons or not will be up to you."

Irene turned to face me. "Lessons?"

I nodded.

"For free?"

"For free or practically nothing. They made it clear this is not something they're doing to get anything from. They're doing it because of you."

My sister seemed dazed by this information and possibly afraid to believe it was true. I tapped her on the shoulder. "Come on now. Get some sleep. In a day or two, I'm sure Mama and Dad will talk to you about it. In a day or two we'll all know more."

Two days later, I found Mama and Cousin Soutine huddled together over tea in the kitchen. I could smell the mint that laced the tea and knew they'd been sitting there a while.

Soutine, who was really a cousin-in-law, was the only one of Mama's cousins who stood out as having a personality of her own. She was taller than the other cousins, a bony, red-haired woman whose white skin stretched like parchment across the angles of her face. She helped out in her husband's delicatessen, which the cousins seemed to tolerate, even though they could become nasty about any Syrian woman who didn't completely devote her life to domestic chores.

After years of hearing Soutine talk to her daughter in a tone even sharper than Mama's tone could be, I came to think of this woman as a red-haired Wicked Witch of the West.

The following day, I came home to change from a skirt I'd gotten dirty when again Soutine's voice pierced the air all the way down the hall. Two visits in a row from this woman was something to be suspicious about. I listened while Soutine questioned Mama in Arabic and Mama sorted out an answer. I couldn't understand Arabic, but it didn't take a genius to listen to the tones of their voices and figure things out.

As soon as I entered the kitchen, the conversation stopped, and Soutine turned her attention to me, her voice changing in tone from sharp to honey-sweet.

I was well aware that Mama hadn't officially said anything to Irene about Mary Ellen's visit and hadn't said anything about the three of us having been invited to go next door for tea. That fact alone should've told me something was up.

5

A week after Mama and I visited with Mary Ellen, I left work early to stop by the house and celebrate Irene's birthday. I'd bought my sister a pink angora sweater as penance for the all the old clothes of mine she had been forced to wear. Mama made a birthday cake and served it at the kitchen table with pistachios and rosewater tea. Dad, of course, wasn't expected home until after seven o'clock.

We cut the cake. I sang "Happy Birthday." Through it all, Irene seemed sad and distracted. When Mama gave her nod of approval, Irene took the paper off my gift, peeled back the white tissue paper, looked at the sweater, then at me with a new, brightened face. "You bought this for me?"

I nodded.

She brushed her fingers across the feather-soft fabric, then lifted the sweater out of the box. She held it up and pressed it to her body. "Is it really mine?"

"Of course! It's your birthday!"

Mama's hand shot out. Her fingers dug into the sweater as if it'd been a present I'd given to her. She yanked the sweater from the box and rubbed the fabric between her fingers, her mouth turning into a sneer.

Mama shoved the sweater back toward Irene. "School girl wear trash?"

"Mama, it's Irene's birthday. She's fifteen years old now. In America, at fifteen they don't dress like little girls."

"Tirteen, I marry. Fourteen, I have child—" Mama's tirade stopped in midstream. She cleared her throat, reached for the sugar, stirred some into her tea, then cleared her throat again producing a sound we knew as a warning of what was to come. "Soon . . ." Mama began.

The clock in the front parlor chimed four o'clock. "Soon Irene be busy after school." Mama took another sip of tea. "Soutine need help wit Antony. She and I talk. Irene help her in the afternoon. Irene learn about children. For woman ting is time Irene should learn."

I pictured Soutine—her pinched mouth, her parchment skin. I pictured her seven-year-old grandson with his sickeningly perfect manners that reminded me of a seventy-year-old man. Of course! Soutine and Mama had been plotting right here in the kitchen—plotting something that would wipe out my sister's opportunity with Mary Ellen and Edna.

I'd always been the rebel in the family—maybe because as an infant I'd suffered terribly with eczema. I'd screamed more than any of the others then, and I've been screaming more than anyone in the family ever since.

"God almighty!" My teacup dropped from my hand as if it were a hot potato. Milky, sugary tea spilled over my skirt, onto the table and splashed onto my shoes and the floor. Before I knew it, I was standing, then yelling, then screaming. "You really can be something, can't you, lady? No wonder you and Soutine were pow-wowing in here the other day!"

Irene stretched her hand toward my arm. "Lottie, no! Lottie don't! Not now! Please don't make a scene!"

I shook away my sister's hand. "No! We're going to have this out once and for all!" I turned my attention back to Mama. "This is why Rose and Belle and Elias don't live here any more! This sneaking around, pretending, denying—while all the time you're working so hard to get exactly what you want!"

Irene was scratching the inside of her lower arm so hard welts had begun to show.

Mama'd turned away from me, her hand rising to her forehead, her mouth turning down at the corners as if she'd been stricken by an unendurable pain.

"Now, Mama, don't start in with the headaches! I know you and that red-haired witch were sitting here cooking up something to prevent your daughter from taking advantage of the opportunity of a lifetime! Mary Ellen said she'd send you an invitation for all of us to come over for tea. Where is it, Mama? Where's the note?"

Before I finished, Mama had closed her eyes, her hand reaching up to clutch her forehead.

"Well? Where is it?"

"Lottie, please! Lottie, don't keep asking her!" Irene had stopped scratching her arm, pressed her hands flat against her ears, and swiveled her body away from us.

"Well?" I said to Mama.

"No unerstand!"

"Oh, stop it! You know enough English to get the butcher at the D.G.S. to cut you the leanest lamb for the lowest price. That means you know when someone brings a note for you to the front door. I bet you got it yesterday or maybe today. Well?"

Mama's hand remained clamped across her forehead.

"Was it yesterday? Today? Come on, Mama. With my own ears, I heard them say they would send you a note with an invitation so the three of us can meet and talk over tea. Mary Ellen's not the kind of lady to make an offer like that and then forget!"

Mama looked at me, her forehead wrinkled in a contrived look of confusion.

"This is your daughter we're talking about, Mama! This is a gift God gave her—not something for you to give or take away! And with or without you, we're going to at least listen to these ladies and hear what they have to say! Now, if you can't remember whether or not you received a note from Mary Ellen, then I'm going to pick up the phone right now and find out!" I took two steps toward the phone in the pantry.

Irene's shoulders hunched forward, her head almost in her lap.

When my arm was two yards from the telephone in the pantry, I heard Mama's grunt as she pushed herself up from her chair.

"I look." She slid off down the front hall, where the sound of rustling near the coatrack was audible. A pocketbook dropped. A change purse clanged to the floor. Both of Irene's hands were under the table, and I could hear the sound of nails scratching against skin.

Mama returned to the kitchen, her hands fumbling with pink paper that had been wadded into a ball. "Dis? Dis some-ting?"

I grabbed the pink stationery and unfolded it, then laid it on the table to smooth out the wrinkles. "Mrs. Awtooah, Edna and I would be delighted if you and your daughters, Lottie and Irene, would come with me to Edna's house for tea on Friday of next week around four o'clock. We look forward to talking to all of you about the matter of lessons for your lovely daughter. If I don't hear from you, we'll be waiting. Sincerely, Your neighbor, Mary Ellen Twitchell."

Mama looked up at me. "Dis it?"

I sank down into my chair and nodded. When I spoke I did my best to soften my tone. "Yes, it is! She's asking us to be there Friday. I'll have to take off early from work, but of course we'll be there."

"You come, too?"

"Of course, I'm coming. I wouldn't miss this for the world!"

Irene had pulled her hands out from under the table. Streaks of red where her nails had been ran diagonally along her arm.

"Come on," I signaled to my sister. "Let's get these dishes done and put the cake away so Dad can have some for dessert when he comes home."

In silence, we washed the few plates and cups. When we were done, Irene walked toward the sweater I had given her and looked toward me as if to ask if she could take it. When I nodded, she put the box in her arms and cradled it as she started down the hall. Then I had a second thought. "Irene! Come back, for a few minutes. There're a few more words I need to say."

I put the kettle on to make Mama another cup of tea. When the tea was ready, I poured Mama a cup and sat down across from her.

Irene sat at the far corner of the table, her chair partly turned toward the hall.

"Now, Mama, don't you think it's possible that taking care of Anthony can wait at least until the end of school?"

Mama's eyes widened, then narrowed as if she were sizing up the best way to finally get what she wanted. "Dis sing lesson—is important?"

"You bet it's important."

I reached for my teacup. The only sounds in the kitchen were Irene's breathing, the ticking of the clock, and my sipping the remainder of my tea.

Mama nodded. "Okay. Do like you say. Take care of An-tony—can wait."

... *6* ...

Three days after Mama agreed to hear what the ladies had to say about lessons for Irene, Mary Ellen walked us to Edna's house, where we would meet to discuss the details. Dressed in a floral print that splashed poppies and lilacs across her ample chest, Mary Ellen accompanied Mama, while I walked beside Irene. Mary Ellen chattered about the noisy Yanchus children and about how late the tulips were to bloom that year. Mama walked and nodded, her eyes directed toward the ground.

Subdued and slender in a white blouse paired with gray slacks that matched the gray-blue of her eyes, Edna O'Malley met us at the front door and greeted us with a warmth I hadn't expected from the "no-nonsense" way she spoke. In the front parlor, she offered us tea biscuits and freshly baked chocolate cake. Tea was poured from a pot on a silver tray. A beautiful piano—a baby grand it must have been—took up one corner of the room.

Mama and I sat on the couch. Irene sat on a facing chair. After tea and cake, Edna asked Irene if she felt ready to try a few songs. "Something from school—something you know, of course." She pulled out a well-worn book of songs. "I'm sure there's something in here you've already sung." She moved to the piano bench and began playing the first chords of several songs. Finally, she found a piece that made Irene nod in time with the music. My sister began to hum the melody and then to sing. Encouraged by Edna's smiles, by the time the song ended, my sister sang with an energy I never knew she had. She even followed Edna's flourish at the end with a trill.

Edna pulled her hands up off the keyboard then broke into applause. Mary Ellen clapped and so did I. Mama clutched the handles of her pocketbook as if she feared either Mary Ellen or Edna might snatch it away.

Edna turned to Irene. "Bravo, my dear! After singing like that you must certainly recognize the importance of developing that voice. Are you willing to give lessons with Mary Ellen and me a try?"

Irene's eyes slipped across the room first to Mama, then to me. I saw one of her hands move toward her lower arm, but she pulled it away. She looked back to Edna. "It's up to Mama, I guess."

Edna flipped several pages in the music book. "Here, we'll convince your mother with this one." Edna swung around to face the piano, and her fingers struck four impressive chords. "Know it?"

Irene smiled and nodded.

The song sounded Spanish—a tune with a snappy rhythm. Irene's eyes shone. Her face became radiant as the song danced along. Hers was no longer the "little sister" voice I heard when she sang with Dad. My sister sang like a woman now. She held herself like a woman—shoulders back, head up, her face transformed by joy. For the first time since she was a child, Irene looked alive, eager, and in love with life.

I found myself swaying and smiling as the song danced to its close. I glanced toward Mama. Her eyes continued their glassy stare. Her hands still clutched the straps of her pocketbook. She seemed to be sinking down into the couch.

When the piece was over, I clapped and jumped up, then ran to embrace my sister, who managed to turn her head away.

"Marvelous! See? I told you, Edna!" Mary Ellen stood up and came over to pat Irene on her shoulder. Then she offered her hand to her friend at the piano. "Well done!"

From her perch on the piano bench, Edna focused her eyes on Mama. "Your daughter shows extraordinary talent, Mrs. Awtooah! But then, seeing as how you have such a musical family, you're probably not surprised. Mary Ellen's told me how beautifully your husband plays his wooden flute! Did he learn that in Syria, where you came from?"

Mama jammed me in the ribs.

"The part of Syria that Mama's from is Lebanon now, Mrs. O'Malley—the part where Mama and Dad came from, anyway," I explained.

Edna reached over to pass the plate of butter cookies to us. I took one. Irene took one, but Mama, who seemed to have sunk farther and farther down into the couch, shook her head.

"We thought that since I live right next to you, Irene could come to my house once or twice a week after school and I could show her . . . well . . ."

". . . the rudiments and essential underpinnings of what might turn out to be an exceptional career," Edna filled in.

"Only an hour a day or so, of course." Mary Ellen added.

"We'll start with terminology—*tempi*, bass clef, treble clef—so she can begin to read notes, then maybe some basic harmony. Does that make sense to you, Mrs. Awtooah?"

Again, Mama's elbow jammed me in the ribs. I settled my teacup back in its saucer. "I'll explain it all to Mama when we get home."

Mary Ellen turned to look at Irene. "How does that sound, Irene? Too much for you to do with school going on? Of course, we can take a rest at any time you need it."

"No. I mean—yes. That sounds fine, Mrs. Twitchell."

"Please call me Mary Ellen, dear. After I help you with the basics, you can walk down here to Edna's house to start on singing lessons—not that you're going to need much instruction."

Edna chimed in, "I hope to mainly offer her encouragement and repertoire. Outside of that, she'll probably be teaching me! Encouragement and repertoire—those are the things she needs from me."

"We certainly want to thank you." I stood up. "We appreciate everything you're trying to do."

"Once you see your way clear to renting a piano if you can, she'll learn quickly. She's such a bright little thing."

I'd never before heard anyone describe my tall sister as a "little thing," but I smiled and helped Mama extricate herself from the couch. "We can pay," I volunteered, although I had no idea whether Mama could or would or how much.

"Edna and I have already talked about that. We'll only need money for whatever music Edna has to buy."

When we got home, I explained things to Mama again. I knew enough not to put her on the spot by asking right then whether she planned to go along with the ladies' idea, so I headed back to work.

That night, I heard Arabic murmurings from my parents' bedroom. Dad and Mama's voices rising, then a long stretch of silence. I heard the English words "piano," "lessons," "neighbor lady," and, of course, Mama's voice slicing sarcastically into the word "Amulcan." Naturally, it would be Mama's voice that spoke the loudest. The children, especially the girls, were strictly Mama's domain—to mold into quiet, obedient, hard-working females who would marry men who could support them so they could create a model family. But that night, underneath Mama's chatter, the quiet baritone of my father's voice persisted.

Three nights later, when I came home from the night shift at work, there stood an upright piano—chipped on the legs and certainly rented, with a bench that didn't match, but the piano and its unmatched bench fit snugly into the far corner of the living room.

"Spensive! Spensive! Irene don't need," Mama probably argued, but Dad must have made one of the few decisions involving his children he's ever made, ending their conversation with the pronouncement that "Piano some-ting Irene should have."

On one of those damp, cool-but-not-cold days that can infuse your body with the delicious nearness of spring, Ralph Alan sat in the courtyard, the blue-and-red check of his shirt the only splash of color in the yard. With his corduroy jacket as ground cover, he'd stretched his legs out and hunched over something Irene was unable to see until she walked over and found that he was chipping away at a block of wood he seemed intent on turning into a four-legged animal. "That's pretty good."

Ralph Alan stopped his chipping. "Nah! This isn't much. You should see the stuff my uncle does." He sat back and inspected his work. "I can't decide whether it's a cat or a cow."

Irene walked back to the bench and opened her loose-leaf notebook. She pulled out a thin, square package wrapped in blue tissue paper and, while Ralph Alan wasn't looking, slipped it behind her back. "Guess which hand. It's something I made for you to thank you for making the plaque with my name. Couldn't get it to you sooner, but go on—guess."

Ralph Alan laid down his knife and the carving. When he pointed to Irene's left hand, she brought out the package and gave it to him. "It's something I made." She nodded toward the package again. "Go on. Open it."

He tore through the paper and laid it on the ground. Under the first piece of tissue paper was a square wrapped in more paper held together with tape.

"Take the tape off. I made two things for you in there."

When he pulled off the tape and the wrapping paper fell to the ground, he saw a drawing of the rectangular slab with Irene's name written on it.

"It even has the bird over there! See?" She pointed to the corner of her drawing. "And there's more. Go to the next one."

A plain white piece of paper came next. Under that was a colored drawing of a male with a crew cut and red cheeks who wore a red-and-blue-checked shirt. His mouth puckered. Music notes streamed from his mouth. In the upper corner of the drawing was a branch that held a bird with a red crest on the top of its head. It, too, had music notes coming from its mouth. In the middle of the paper, the notes from the boy and the bird came together. Underneath, Irene had written: "Ralph Alan and His Friend."

Ralph Alan peered closely at the picture, held it at arm's length then brought it close, his brows coming together in a frown.

"You don't like it."

"I do! Really! I've never had a real drawing done of me before. I didn't know you could draw."

"I did five of them before I got it right."

He held the drawing at arm's length again and smiled. "It's the nicest present I ever got."

While Ralph Alan folded the paper back around the drawings, Irene walked across the courtyard and knelt beside the leaf-covered slab of concrete and brushed away the leaves.

"Ralph Alan, can I ask you something?"

"Sure."

"It's none of my business, and you don't have to tell me if you don't want to." She waited for a reaction, but there was none. "I've been wondering . . . I mean . . . well . . . is it true you once hurt your pop pretty bad?"

Ralph Alan leaned his head back against the trunk of the tree. He closed his eyes. "Weren't nothing else I could do." With his eyes still closed, he frowned as if trying to remember exactly the way it had been. "It's not right for a man to be hitting on a woman and a little girl. Jo Ellen and Mama . . . they were so scared that night."

"Did you pray to God not to punish you for what you did?"

"God loves us no matter what we do, Irene. He knows Pop never hurt anyone before he lost his job and got sugar diabetes and started in with the drinking, but Pop was hurting Jo Ellen and Mama real bad that night."

Irene reached for some fallen leaves, crumbled them, then let them fall to the ground. "But Mama says God will punish me for not dusting my room or cleaning the dishes right."

Ralph Alan shook his head. "I've told you. He's not that kind of God, Irene. He's not. " With a nod of his head to punctuate the "not," Ralph Alan picked up his knife and returned to chipping wood.

They sat in silence until an airplane droned overhead, and they looked up to watch it dip into a circle over the Potomac before moving south toward the airport.

Irene spoke first after the plane had disappeared. "Sometimes, when I'm in my room, I look out at the river and wish I could swim right into the middle of it or float up into the blueness of the sky—to be somewhere safe where everything's quiet and safe and fine—to a place that looks like it does where the clouds meet the river."

Without looking up from his whittling, Ralph Alan nodded. Several minutes later, the university bells announced the time, and Irene jumped up. "Four o'clock! I've gotta go!" She gathered her schoolbooks and juggled them with one hand. With the other hand, she buttoned up her coat.

She hurried toward the corridor entrance, then turned. "It doesn't matter about hurting your pop, Ralph Alan, and I'm glad God didn't punish you. You did a brave thing that day, and I'm really, really glad that you're my friend."

$$\ldots\,7\,\ldots$$

Piano lessons with Mary Ellen began the third week of April. Twice a week, Irene spent forty-five minutes at her house learning the basics. Thirty minutes were put aside each day for practicing. Each weekday, my sister moved her fingers up and down the keyboard in what Mary Ellen called "the building-block scales." After a month, she began playing melodies with one hand. Even as she repeated these boring sounds, my sister's spirits seemed to soar.

As Irene practiced, Mama stormed from room to room, polishing, dusting, and scrubbing, thudding her feet as she clamored up and down the stairs. She scrubbed dishes as if food particles had to be erased from the face of the earth and rubbed clothes against the washboard until I thought they would shred.

One evening, when I met Irene in the upstairs hall, I asked her how the piano lessons were going. She pulled me into her room and closed the door. "Mary Ellen's wonderful, Lottie! She really listens to me! And sometimes Edna comes over and tells stories about famous singers who sing all over the world. They play records for me to listen to, and when I make a mistake—can you imagine? Mary Ellen doesn't scold at all!"

A month after lessons started, when I told Mama that Mary Ellen said Irene's musical talent was special enough for her to have a singing career, Mama's face settled into a stunned, far-away look similar to one I'd seen in pictures of children in bombed-out cities after a war.

. . .

Irene's first singing lesson was to take place after school let out in early June. In the meantime, she sandwiched piano lessons and daily practice in between completing enough homework to get by at school and dusting and ironing and hanging clothes out to dry.

Twice before the end of May, at Ralph Alan's suggestion, Irene met him at the street side of Georgetown's Visitation Convent grounds.

Visitation Convent was a private girls' school eight blocks from Mama's house. Its property consisted of acres of immaculately tended hills separated by a wrought-iron fence that seemed to say: *Private! This place is for rich girls only.* The grounds were immaculate—the grass was a green velvet carpet in the sun. Gardeners tended seasonal flowers throughout the year.

On this particular day, wild roses sprayed leafy green tendrils over the fences on the street sides of the grounds. Ralph Alan balanced himself on the bottom rung of the fence and looked out toward the grass and hills. He gestured to Irene to join him.

She shook her head and remained where she was.

"But you can't see what the whole place looks like from where you are. Come on. Step up here. You won't fall. Is that what you're afraid of?"

She shook her head. "It's just that I don't like fences—not ones with pointy iron tops like these."

He beckoned her over and held out his hand. "Come on, just for a minute. You really can't see the place from over there."

Irene hesitated, then walked toward Ralph Alan and let him take her hand.

"Step up and hold on from here." He pointed to a thick vertical post and steadied her with his hand. She slipped one foot onto the bottom wrought-iron rail, held tightly to Ralph Alan's outstretched hand, then stepped up with her other foot.

"There! Isn't that something? Reminds me of my uncle's farm."

Together they looked out onto acres of grass. Ralph Alan pointed out the spires of nearby Georgetown University. They fell silent, listening to the distant clang of a trolley, the rumble of a passing bus.

After Ralph Alan stepped back off the railing, he helped Irene down, then walked to a small rise in the land about ten feet away from the fence, lay back and rested his head on the open palms of his hand, then closed his eyes. Bees hummed around a lilac bush that glowed in the three o'clock sun. The air was fresh with the smell of acres of newly cut grass.

Irene began collecting dandelions, tucked a yellow bouquet into her pocket, and walked over to sit several feet from Ralph Alan. "Do you think God knows I'm happy? Can He know I've got the piano and lessons, too? Can He be with me here right now and also at home with Mama, too?"

"Sure He can. He can see your mama and your pop and you and me. God can see it all."

She picked a buttercup and twirled it first one way then the other. "When I'm in my room, I can stand on my bed and see a tiny part of the Potomac River. Sometimes I wish I could swim into the middle of it, then float right up into the sky. Can God see me when I'm in my room? Can He see way down into the ocean and into the river and the sea?"

Ralph Alan sat up, folded his legs Indian style, and plucked randomly at blades of grass. "Uncle told me to think of God swimming through all of it out there—swimming and looking, swimming and looking—all over this great big world He's made."

"And He hears me when I sing?"

"Of course He does."

Irene brought her knees close to her chest, carefully tucking the skirt of her dress around her legs. "How do we get to see Him, Ralph Alan? If He lives way up there, how do we get to see Him when we die?"

Ralph Alan fell back on the ground and brought his hands up underneath his head. "Well . . . what I think is . . ." he paused, bunched his lips together then frowned. "I think that maybe when we die, we're spilled out into all that open space of heaven—like the water of the river except it reaches way up high into the sky."

He pushed himself up to sit, leaned his head to one side as if he were evaluating his answer. "Yep. I think that's it. And then when we're up there, we're supposed to spread our arms and start doing like this—" he made breaststroke swimming motions with his arms, "—kinda like that. If God is like one of those lighthouse lights like my uncle says He is, then we just look toward the brightest place and keep swimming toward the light."

The third week of June turned hotter than a day in July. On the night before Irene's first singing lesson, all bedroom doors were left wide open to circulate any speck of cooler air. That night at dinner, the more Irene pushed her plate of food away, the more shrilly Mama yelled, "*Killeh!* Eat! You gonna be skin 'n' bone!"

In the morning, showers filled the predawn hours. The day dawned cooler, but by eleven o'clock, the temperature rose to eighty degrees.

Mama had stayed up until midnight adding a strip of embroidered lace to a green-and-white ten-year-old Easter dress of mine. At eight o'clock, she supervised the washing of my sister's hair, cleaned underneath Irene's nails, then ordered Irene to sit for thirty minutes in the sun— "for color in face."

At 12:45, Mama inspected Irene, pinched her cheeks for added color, licked her forefinger and ran it along each of Irene's eyebrows, patting them down. She had stuffed herself into a long-sleeved plaid cotton dress, black stockings and laced-up black shoes. Both pockets bulged with white paper napkins. She looped her arm through the twin cracked leather straps of her one black pocketbook, and in her hands, she carried a plate of Syrian sweet cakes made of baked farina, cinnamon, and ground nuts and dusted with powdered sugar. She held the plate in front of her as if it were a plate of royal treats.

"You tink she like?" Mama asked Irene.

Irene nodded once, then looked down at her fingers as they picked at the cuticles of her nails until Mama's elbow jabbed at Irene's side. "Stop dat! *Maj-noon-eh?* You crazy?"

They walked the four blocks in silence, stepping around puddles left by last night's rain, Mama with chin up and jutting forward, Irene with head down, feet scuffing along the ground. On Mrs. O'Malley's porch,

Mama rested the plate of cookies on the arm of a chair and reached out to smooth down the wrinkles from the skirt of Irene's dress and indicated that Irene should ring the doorbell.

When she came to the door, Edna O'Malley beamed at Irene, then focused on Mama. "Mrs. Awtooah! I didn't think you'd come, too. I'd planned—I mean I'd thought Irene and I would start her first few lessons alone."

Mama shifted the plate into one hand and dug into a pocket for one of her paper napkins. She pulled it out, crumpled it in her hand then stuffed it back into her pocket. The cookies remained perfectly balanced a foot and a half below Edna's nose.

"Oh, my! You brought a treat! Is this for me?"

Mama nodded then lifted up the plate like an offering.

"They look scrumptious! What a thoughtful thing for you to do!" She motioned Irene into the house. "Go on. Put them on the kitchen table, will you, Irene?" Edna stepped back to let Irene pass.

Irene hesitated, turned toward Mama but did not look into her eyes. Mama started to follow her daughter into the house, but Edna stepped forward, effectively barring Mama from the house. "I'm awfully sorry, Mrs. Awtooah. I guess I didn't say it plain enough. I want to start these lessons with Irene alone—to make her feel comfortable with me. Maybe you can sit in on a lesson in a month or so—after we've gotten underway. You understand?"

Mama's eyes registered the surprise of one who'd been stung by a bee. Edna waited until, eventually, Mama answered with a nod.

"Don't you worry now. She won't be gone all that long. Thanks so much for the goodies! I'll be sure she gets home safe and sound!"

After Edna stepped back and closed the door, Mama remained facing the door that had been closed in front of her. She pulled out a paper napkin and dabbed it to the skin above her upper lip then stuffed the napkin back into the pocket of her sweater.

Piano music came from inside the house—then the sound of female voices laughing. Mama stood at the edge of the stairs that led down to the sidewalk and stared toward the shuttered houses across the street. She reached out for the railing, then looked back toward the house from which the sound of her daughter's laughter came.

When she eventually grasped the railing, she lumbered down the stairs, descending one step at a time.

On the sidewalk, she curled up her arm to let her pocketbook settle into the crook of her elbow. The hand of that arm became a fist that she pressed into a place below her breast. At the curb, she looked left, then right—more as if she'd forgotten something than to look out for passing cars. She stepped down into the street, splashing her skirt with the muddy water of a puddle. Water dripped from the hem of her skirt and still she did not move. One car from the left passed her, then two from the right. She remained standing in the street.

A young man passed her, turned, walked back, and touched her on the arm. "You all right, lady? You want help?"

Mama nodded to the first question, then shook her head and yanked her arm holding the pocketbook closer to her body.

"Cars come mighty fast around this corner. You better watch out."

Mama stared straight ahead.

"Sure you're not lost?"

After Mama shook her head again, the man shrugged and walked away. Mama pushed one foot in front of the other across the cobblestone pavement. At the curb, her foot splashed into another puddle. She stepped up, oblivious to the stain widening along the bottom of her skirt and to the water that spotted her black stockings.

On the sidewalk, she straightened her arm so the straps of her pocketbook slid into her hand. She looked down at her pocketbook while her fingers fumbled with the clasp.

For several minutes, Mama stood at the corner with both hands holding her pocketbook close to the front of her body, her eyes focusing on nothing as she stared straight ahead. It was as if, without Irene beside her, she couldn't remember which way led to her home.

.   .   .

During the early part of that summer, Mama let Irene practice her piano and her singing without interruption, but after Mama finished scrubbing the kitchen floor, sweeping the hall, or washing the front steps and the back, she'd stand at the entrance to the front parlor, dabbing at her checks and her forehead with a napkin, fanning herself by flapping her apron toward her face. Sometimes, after Irene had been practicing only ten or fifteen minutes, Mama would yell, "You done?" or "Be done soon?"

From time to time, I'd remember to ask how things were going with Irene, and Mama would answer with something like, "Amulcan lady live two blocks away," or "*judrah* for dinner. When you be home?"—responses that had no relation to the question I'd asked.

On a particularly hot July day when bees hummed around clusters of black-eyed Susans, Irene carried a sack of groceries into the courtyard and found Ralph Alan bent over his carving, which now had two ears and the beginning of a tail. She set down the bag of groceries, raised her arms toward the sky, and twirled completely around.

"Do you believe it? Edna says I'm good enough to give a recital sometime next year. And they're saying when they've taught me all they know, maybe I can study singing at Peabody in Baltimore!" She walked to a cluster of dandelions and picked one with a halo of feathery seeds. She shut her eyes, blew on the dandelion, opened her eyes, saw that seeds still clung to the stalk, and tossed the flower away. "Did you ever have a girlfriend, Ralph Alan?"

Ralph Alan folded in the blades of his knife and put it in his back pocket. "Nope."

"Never?"

"I tried to put my arm around Marlene Tolsen once at the Saturday movies."

"And what happened?"

"She moved two seats away. Toby's the one with the girlfriends."

"I don't like Toby."

"Toby's all right." Ralph Alan blew wood shavings from his carving, then brushed off his pants. "He'll be starting to take care of Pop—now that I'm going to be going away."

"Away?"

"My uncle needs me for the rest of the summer at the farm."

"The rest of the summer?"

"And maybe into the fall."

"All the way into fall?"

"Maybe."

"How soon are you leaving?"

"Pretty soon—whenever I can get a ride."

"Tomorrow?"

He frowned. "Not that soon—I don't think."

"Will you let me know?"

"I wouldn't leave without saying good-bye."

Irene picked up her groceries. "Well, I'll just pretend that you're not going away until I hear from you. That way I won't feel so sad."

When Irene reached the tunnel leading to the street, Ralph Alan called out. "Irene? God wants you to be happy. And I don't ever want to be the one to make you sad."

. . . 8 . . .

In the days after her first singing lesson, Irene hummed while drying dishes, played the piano whenever she had a minute, and sang to herself nearly all the time. She volunteered to iron Dad's shirts, scrub dirtied pots and pans, and even wash the upstairs windows. Abruptly, at the end of July, Irene hardly sang at all. She didn't practice the piano, started missing her lessons, and Mama had to yell to get her to make her bed.

Near the end of July, as dusk brought on the first coolness of the day, I stood on the back porch looking up at the outline of the crescent moon and caught the shape of shoulders hunched forward out of the corner of my eye. Irene sat on the lowest step with her legs bunched close to her chest.

"You dreaming about a concert at Constitution Hall?"

Irene looked up, shook her head then leaned forward again to rest her cheek on her knee.

Above us, dusty pink fingers in the sky gave way to gray. I moved so that a wedge of light from the kitchen would fall on Irene's face. What I saw was the loneliness I'd seen in the faces of female customers at the restaurant who came before dark to drink alone at the bar. I reached out to touch Irene's shoulder, but she pulled away.

"Sweetheart, what's the matter? You can tell me."

She raised her head as if it had been weighted down with the worries of the world. I saw the glistening of tears in her eyes. "He's going away."

"Who? Who's going away?"

"Ralph Alan."

"Ralph Alan Yanchus? You mean Ralph Alan Yanchus from down the street? The one you met in the courtyard at the beginning of school?"

She nodded.

"You go on dates?"

"Oh, no! Nothing like that! We just sit in the courtyard mostly and talk about squirrels and birds and trees and even about God."

"But Ralph Alan's got to be seventeen, eighteen by now."

"Eighteen last January." she offered. "And he's going away to help out at his uncle's farm—maybe for more than a month. Ralph Alan Yanchus is my friend." She searched my eyes as if to determine whether I could understand.

This new information required that I look at my sister as if I'd never seen her before. This was not Irene, my baby sister, but a young woman who talked to Ralph Alan Yanchus, the blond, red-cheeked bear of a boy from down the street—except Ralph Alan was no longer a boy.

I looked at Irene again. Too tall, yes. Too thin. But her thinness had a delicacy that reminded me of a birch tree standing alone—slender and graceful, well on her way to becoming a woman, and quite possibly desperate with the need for love. "Well, if he's your friend, I'm sure Ralph Alan will come back home before too long."

Irene hugged her knees more tightly. "It's just that when you like someone special, you never know if they're ever going to be coming back when they go away."

"Did he say he wasn't coming back?"

Irene shook her head and began scratching the inside of her lower arm.

I tried to block out the rasp of nails against skin. I thought what it must be like to grow into a young woman with Mama as the only constant person in your life, about being doomed to being laughed at by schoolmates who looked at you as "odd"—or, even worse, to be ignored. I thought about high school locker room discussions of parties and Friday night dances lead by shiny-haired blondes in cheerleader sweaters who talked as if this dark-skinned, tall, lanky Arab wasn't even in the room.

I leaned forward and touched my sister on her shoulder. "Would you like to go to the movies with me as soon as I can get a day off? There's a good one down at the Calvert—Danny Kaye and Virginia Mayo. It'll be good for you to laugh."

"No thanks. I don't like the movies much."

"Well, is there something you would like to do? Something to get away from the house for a while?"

She thought for a minute, then her face lit up for the first time that evening. "The zoo. I'd really like to visit the zoo."

"Well—okay. I guess we could go there even though it's not my favorite place—all those animal smells! But we'll go after Ralph Alan leaves, if that's what you want."

"Thank you, Lottie. Thank you so much for trying to understand."

A week after Ralph Alan announced he'd be going away, on a day so hot and humid it felt as if steam filled up the air, Irene found her friend in the courtyard squatting next to the concrete slab that bore her name. He spoke without looking up. "I did it pretty good, wouldn't you say?"

"You did. You really did."

Ralph Alan stood up and reached into his pocket. He pulled out something wrapped in a blue-and-white handkerchief. He held it in front of him with two hands, shifted his weight and cleared his throat. "Tomorrow. It's tomorrow, I'm going away."

"Right now? In this heat?"

"This heat's nothing—nothing like it can get on the farm."

"Is working on a farm hard?"

"I guess so. It feels good, though—at the end of the day, you know you've done something!"

The university clock rang one, then two, three, then four. Ralph Alan shoved the handkerchief-wrapped bundle in front of Irene. "Here. Take it. It's only a start, but I thought you'd like it anyway. I'll be doing more of them at the farm."

"For me? You want to give it to me?"

Ralph Alan nodded and pushed the bundle into her hands.

Irene began to unfold its cotton cover.

"Why don't you wait 'til you get home to look it over."

"No. I want to see it now!" She folded back the cotton and held out the carving to inspect. "Why, it's a kind of cat-dog-cow!" She rubbed her hand along the carving's back and sides. "I didn't know wood could feel this smooth! Thank you so much! I'll keep it and touch it, and it'll help a little now that you'll be gone."

Tenderly, she wrapped the carving back in the handkerchief. Then, holding the carving in both hands, she walked toward the entrance to the street. Before her body was swallowed up by the tunnel's shadows, she paused and turned. "I'll miss you, Ralph Alan."

From behind her, as she walked through the semidark of the tunnel came the words, "Take care of yourself, Irene," but Irene was already too close to the street to hear.

At home, Irene tucked the carving, still wrapped in the handkerchief, in the back of the bottom drawer of her dresser. She slept with it under her pillow for a month until one day she forgot to remove it in the morning, and by bedtime that night the carving was gone.

The weather had cooled off on the day Irene and I headed to the Washington Zoo. We took the streetcar, then the bus and got off at the Connecticut Avenue entrance.

My sister ran ahead of me through the wrought-iron gates. She ran straight down the entrance path, then stopped and looked around as if she were Dorothy arriving in the Land of Oz. "Listen, Lottie! Listen to all the birds!"

She looked as if she could stand still listening for the rest of the day. "Yes, they're nice, but we'd better get started if we're going to fit most of it in."

"Not most of it! I want to see all of it!"

"The zoo's much bigger than it looks. You really are going to have to choose what you want to see."

My sister chose the zebras first—"because they have to live so far, far away from home. How can they do it? How come they don't just die living so awfully far away from home?"

"Even if they were born in Africa, they were tiny little babies when they came here. Besides, it was a long time ago. Animals can't remember far away like that."

Irene gave me a doubtful look as she began to move along. "But animals can dream."

"I doubt it."

"Ralph Alan once told me about a dog he had that would go to sleep, and, with his eyes closed, he'd pretend to snap at flies. If animals can dream, maybe they dream about their home."

"This is their home. Come on. Let's get a move on."

Outside the enclosure for the bears, Irene tossed unshelled peanuts across the fence.

"Irene, you're not supposed to feed them! Look at the sign!"

"But they're hungry, Lottie!"

"The zoo pays people who are trained to feed the animals—that's what a zoo is all about. They have specialists here who know exactly what the animals need."

Irene pitched her last two peanuts over the fence. "But suppose they just put the food down in front of them and walk away! Animals need to be petted. They do! They really do!"

I walked over to Irene and took her hand. "But feeding them is not our job. Come on. My stomach says it's time for a hot dog and a Coke."

She pulled her hand away. "I'm not hungry. I want to see the lions. You go on. I'll meet you by the lions when you're done. I promise."

Twenty minutes later, when I returned, she was standing at the fence in front of the lions.

"Why don't we see some other animals now? Mama will be worried if we don't get home before four."

My sister lingered. "But they're so sad. Look how they keep looking so far away. All locked up like that and they can't go anywhere on their own. They just stand and stare into nothing like they're going to sleep inside."

I hadn't seen Irene as passionate about something since I watched her when she sang at Edna's. I rested my hand on her arm. "That's the way it is for them, Irene. They get used to it, I'm sure." I turned her gently away. "Let's see the giraffes and that cute new monkey before it's time to go."

Three nights after our trip to the zoo, on an evening when the heat pressed in on all sides, Mama pulled me aside after dishes had been washed and turned to face me, her mouth scrunched down at the corners with that determined look she can get. "What you tink about Irene sing? Is some-ting good?"

I knew from the way she asked the question that Mama didn't want an honest answer, so I shrugged and said nothing.

"Irene not know how take care house, children—not know what woman need to do." Without waiting for an answer, Mama thumped across the kitchen floor, untied her apron, and hung it on the hook. When she turned to face me, her eyes focused on a place beside the corner of my mouth—exactly where she looks when she's about to say something she knows I'm not going to like. Her chin jutted forward as she said, "Irene need learn woman ting. For An-tony now is time."

I hated Mama's way of sneaking up on you from behind before she hits you over the head with her latest proclamation. I seriously started to ask myself how much longer I could stand living in that house. I began to think that living at home to save money for secretarial school was not worth the price. It wasn't so much watching Mama direct my sister's life that bothered me as the fact that she was asking my sister to bury a very special gift from God. That frightened me more than I could say.

What kept me from packing up my belongings right after Mama's latest pronouncement was the reappearance of Cousin Freddie.

Freddie Kiatta was a distant cousin who'd been stationed at Fort Myer. What I particularly remember is that Freddie used to stop by for a short visit and then would inevitably stay for Mama's *kibbeh* or her dumplings in a garlic-yogurt sauce. And he was the only person I knew who could tell a joke that actually made Mama laugh. After dinner, he would make time for a game of checkers with Dad and always had time to ask me how I was doing in school, listening to my answer with a twinkle in his eye that told me he knew there was more to the story than I was telling.

Two days after Mother's pronouncement about Irene's babysitting with Anthony, Freddie rang Mama's doorbell when three cousins were visiting. Freddie's hair was now peppered with strands of gray, but, thank God, he didn't try to tame its waves with tonic or grease. Freddie arrived that day with boxes of tinned sweets straight from Lebanon as if he had known several cousins would be there—or possibly he was simply a generous person, which, I was to find out later, was true.

After he'd distributed the sweets, he presented Mama with a beautiful hammered brass tray—"from the old country," he made a point of saying. When she realized it was for her, the dimples that we rarely saw appeared in Mama's cheeks.

Within fifteen minutes, Freddie had taken orders for ice cream cones and had persuaded Irene to go with him to Sugar's Drugstore to help carry the cones back to Mama's. When they returned, my sister was laughing with a delight I rarely saw before she met Ralph Alan and certainly never expected to see this soon after he'd gone away. My sister walked in with her own double-dip cone—one scoop of peach and one scoop of chocolate chip—a more daring combination than I'd seen her choose before.

Freddie stayed for more than an hour, joking with Mama and the ladies, in Arabic, of course. When Freddie said "good-bye" and headed down the hall to the front door, he left me with a comfortable feeling, possibly because he was genuinely sweet to these women who were starved for caring male attention. It seemed to me that Cousin Freddie might be one of a truly rare species—a male unafraid of letting his gentleness show through.

... 9 ...

The following Saturday, by the time Mama and Irene had walked the four blocks to where Irene was to have her first babysitting experience with Soutine's grandson, the temperature had already climbed to ninety degrees. An early morning shower had turned the heat into a steam bath. Twice, Irene stopped to lift her hair from her neck, fanning her skin with her other hand, and each time, Mama grabbed Irene's hand and pulled her on.

A little after nine, they stood at the bottom of the stairs of Cousin Usma's house. Mama took out a napkin and patted the sweat that dripped down the side of her face. She reached out to the railing, put one foot on the bottom stair, then looked up at Soutine, the bony woman who waited for them at the top of the steps with her arms folded across her chest. Dressed and ready to walk the ten blocks to her husband's store, Anthony's grandmother waited as Mama climbed the stairs. When Mama reached the top stair, she glared back at Irene and beckoned her to hurry. *"Y'allah!"*

Irene dipped her head in response, pushed her feet forward, and trudged up the stairs.

Soutine marched over to Irene, clamped her hand around Irene's jaw, and, since she was shorter than my sister, forced Irene's face down in order to peer into her face. She looked over her shoulder to Mama. "You tink she can do?"

Mama nodded. "She do. She learn."

The two women walked to the far corner of the porch and murmured in Arabic, glancing back occasionally toward Irene. Then Soutine picked up her pocketbook and marched to the edge of the porch, patted her hat as if giving orders for it to stay on her head, tossed one look back at Irene, and descended to the street.

Mama took out another napkin, unbuttoned the top two buttons of her dress, and mopped the sweat that had gathered there. She pointed toward the screen door, indicating that Irene should walk in that direction.

Waiting in the hallway shadows was the outline of a boy. The outline pushed the door open and seven-year-old Anthony, dressed in knee pants, bow tie, and white long-sleeved shirt, walked toward Irene. His skin was powdery white like his grandmother's. Chestnut hair with highlights of red was slicked back from his forehead with something that gave it a greasy shine. His blue-gray eyes inspected Irene. Like a toy soldier, he shot out his hand for Irene to shake. "I'm Anthony. We're supposed to play in the basement. I'm supposed to lead the way."

He pivoted on his heels, held the screen door open for Irene and Mama, then led them through the first floor hallway of Cousin Usma's house, where Anthony came after school on days when his grandmother helped out at her husband's store. As if he'd rehearsed this scene many times, Anthony opened the door to the basement, reached on tiptoe for the light, and led Irene down the stairs.

Within minutes, Irene and Anthony were seated in repainted kitchen chairs around a card table that had been patched with gray tape. Above them, a lone lightbulb hung on a metal chain. A coloring book lay open on the table, a box of crayons next to it. Anthony leaned forward and inspected the half-colored page of an airplane. He flipped the pages in the coloring book, then turned back to the half-colored plane.

When Anthony reached for the crayon box, Irene already had the box in her hand and was starting to shake the crayons out, but Anthony's hand shot forward to stop her. "No! Taiteh says 'no crayons on the table.' " He grabbed the box and tapped the crayons back inside.

"But you can't see what you've got! Look at all these wonderful colors! There's no way you can really choose!"

He shrugged and pulled out one crayon, inspected it, put it back, slipped out another, tested it, then put that one back. He repeated this four times until he'd found a color that seemed to be right. He bent over his work, his hand holding the crayon with three middle fingers coming together to oppose his thumb, as if he were eating with chopsticks instead of coloring the outline of a plane. When he finished the picture of the airplane, he flipped through the pages until he found a picture of a car.

Irene pushed back her chair and started to stand, but before she was on her feet, Anthony reached out for her arm. "Since it's Cousin Usma's house, Taiteh said we have to sit right here at this table. Taiteh said not to touch anything."

Irene pulled her hand away, stood up. "I'm not going to touch anything! It's just that it's so dark down here, I'm not going to even be able to see!" She walked over to the basement's two rectangular half-windows that let in light from the street. Turning back toward the table, she sneezed, then sneezed again.

Like a soldier jumping to attention, Anthony stood up, reached into his pocket, and shot out a hand that held a neatly folded handkerchief. Irene looked down at the square of white cotton and shook her head. She reached into her skirt pocket, pulled out a napkin and blew her nose. Anthony shrugged and sat down. He pulled out a brown crayon and began coloring the car.

Irene sat down, leaned her elbows on the table, and watched Anthony draw. "Why don't you make the car yellow? The latest Studebaker that came out is yellow! Have you seen it?"

He shook his head. "I think yellow cars are stupid. Cars should be dark green or gray or brown or black." He sat back, studied the picture, frowned, then picked up a yellow crayon to color in the sun. When he'd finished his coloring, he looked at his coloring again, slipped the crayon back in place, then leaned forward, tore the crayoned picture out of the book, and shoved the finished product toward Irene. "Here." He flapped the picture at Irene again. "I'm supposed to give you whatever I finish so you can take it home."

Irene took the picture, looked at it, then pushed it back across the table. "Put your name down in the corner. That's what artists do."

"Why?"

"Because."

Anthony frowned. "Taiteh says 'because' isn't a good enough reason."

"What about your mother? Doesn't she ever have anything to say?"

Anthony's eyebrows came together in a look that showed his anger at Irene's question. "Don't you know? Mama works a lot, and Taiteh's the one who tells us what to do. Taiteh tells us how things've gotta be."

Irene frowned. "Well, I want to put your picture up in my room. I like your picture, and I want your name on it."

"You don't really like the picture. You're just saying that to be nice."

"I like it, Anthony!" She spoke more softly this time. "I like it because you gave it to me."

He looked doubtfully at Irene, then reached toward the crayon box, selected a dark blue crayon, leaned over the paper, and spent a full minute shaping the seven letters of his name. He handed her the picture, sat back, then fixed his eyes on the birthmark on Irene's neck. A finger shot out in her direction. "You got a dirty place on your neck right there."

Irene pulled her head back. "It's a birthmark. God gave it to me the day I was born."

"Can I touch it? Does it hurt?"

"No it doesn't hurt and . . ." she thought for a moment. "No, you can't touch it right now."

"Can I ever?"

"Depends."

"On what?"

"On if you do what I tell you to when I'm here."

He eyed her suspiciously, then pulled back the cuff of his shirtsleeve and checked the watch on a black wristband that overwhelmed the thin bones of his arm. "Taiteh said for the first time that forty-five minutes would be okay. That means we've done enough. Now we can have cookies and milk upstairs." He stood up, carefully closed the crayon box, tucked the box and the coloring book under his arm, and started up the stairs. Halfway up the stairs, he turned back to look at Irene, who was three steps below him. "Did it hurt when God gave you the mark on your neck?"

"How would I know? I had it when I was born."

"Is it a punishment?"

"Stop asking questions! Mama and Cousin Usma are waiting." Irene gestured with her hand. "Now get on up the stairs!"

Obediently, Anthony climbed the last four steps. At the top, without turning around, he said, "There goes Anthony—asking too many questions again." He opened the kitchen door and held it open until Irene walked through.

Even with Ralph Alan's being away, Irene stopped by the courtyard whenever Mama sent her to Sugar's Drugstore or the D.G.S. or to a cousin's down the street. Once inside the courtyard and satisfied she was alone, she usually walked straight to the place where her name lay buried under leaves.

Sometimes she sat on a bench, closed her eyes, and pictured each letter of her name as Ralph Alan had carved it into the concrete slab. Other times, she brushed aside the leaves, traced the letters of her name, singing them on random notes of the scale. Always, she pictured Ralph Alan—Ralph Alan pursing his lips to answer the trill of a bird or Ralph Alan with hands folded behind his head, his back leaning against a tree.

Ralph Alan had been gone for three weeks on a day Irene emerged from the courtyard to head for home, and Toby Yanchus, who'd cut off the bottom of Irene's dress in middle school, slipped out from the other side of the six-foot hedge.

When she saw him, Irene took one step backward.

"Hi ya!" Toby grinned, stepped closer, jamming his hands in his pockets and jingling loose change.

Irene flicked her eyes to Toby's pockets—first his right then his left. She snapped her head around toward the tunnel as if to check on whether she should run back into the courtyard.

One of Toby's hands emerged from his trouser pocket. "Here. Something my brother sent." He opened his palm to reveal a folded up sheet of lined paper. "Go on. Take it. My brother's last letter to Ma said 'give this to Irene up the street.' "

Irene put the grocery bag she was carrying on the sidewalk and took the note and unfolded it. "Won't be home till after September some time." The note was not signed.

Irene read it again, then crumpled the note in her hand.

"Whatcha do that for?" Toby jammed his hands inside his trouser pockets and shrugged. "Suit yourself." He started down the street then stopped and looked back at Irene. "Hey, you two aren't 'doing it,' are you? That'd be something, wouldn't it? Irene Awtooah and Ralph Alan the saint?"

Irene's eyes widened as if a three-headed monster had dropped down from the sky.

"Okay! Okay! Just teasing. Don't get crazy on me now!" He walked away, jingling the change in his pocket.

Irene stood still and watched his retreat. Then she looked down at the crumpled paper in her hand, smoothed it out, and began the two-block walk toward home.

10

Mama's energy had flagged in the days just after Irene's first singing lessons in July, but by the week before the family picnic on Labor Day weekend, she was a whirling tornado from morning until night.

Twice, I had to take the bus across town to the Syrian grocery store for extra wheat for the *tabbouleh,* for rose water for the farina and nut cookies, and for the spice Mama called *mahleb,* the nutty flavoring she used in her date and farina cakes.

Picnic baskets and special checked tablecloths had to be resurrected. Wheat had to be soaked. Excursions to Neam's market on Wisconsin Avenue had to be planned in order to purchase all the extra items the D.G.S would never be able to supply—jars of grape leaves, sacks of potatoes, ten bunches of parsley, and bags of pistachios that had to be shelled and ground.

Married sons and daughters were asked to drive the older relatives who didn't own cars. In order to avoid bringing up ancient family antagonisms, rides had to be carefully engineered. Two weeks earlier, Mama enlisted Freddie's help in planning who would ride with whom because he seemed to have a remarkable memory for ancient family slights and hurts. Mama even persuaded Freddie to help roll and stuff the grape leaves—a job I could no more imagine Dad undertaking than I could see his walking on the moon.

On Saturday before the picnic, I took off work early. Food had to be distributed to the ten cars that were going. Dry ice had to be purchased along with bags and bags of regular ice, which were stored in refrigerators up and down Prospect Street. Gallons of iced tea with mint and lemon had to be prepared. Over a hundred cubes of lamb had to be cut and marinated in a bath of bay leaf, oregano, garlic, onion, and red wine.

After Mama and Dad had gone to sleep Saturday night, I was sitting in Dad's rocking chair on the porch when I heard a rustling in the lilac bush and the sound of sniffling.

"Irene?" I waited, then whispered her name again. Eventually, my sister emerged. When I beckoned her to sit next to me on the stairs, she inched forward and sat down.

"Got the jitters about tomorrow's big family event?" I tried to drape my arm around her shoulder, but she pulled away. "I used to hate these things when we were kids."

She didn't answer.

"Maybe it'll rain tomorrow," I said.

"I don't want Mama to think I'm ungrateful. I know she wants so much for me to be like my cousins, but every time I'm with them, I just don't belong!"

How I wished I could say to her, "Mama wants you to be just the way you are!" But I wasn't capable of telling that lie.

I thought about the time at Edna's when I'd first heard the magic of my sister's singing voice. She'd not only sung the music—she'd lived it. What did the giggling teenaged Syrian girls who would be at the picnic know about such intensity and passion? Mainly, these girls gossiped about which boy might ask them to dance at the St. George's Friday night social and about the gossip in the latest movie magazines.

I leaned forward to touch my sister's shoulder. "The right place will come for you—the right place and time and the right friends. It will."

How miserable she'd be as the wife of a Syrian storekeeper's son! Diapering babies, cooking, doing housework so it would meet the standards of the outside world while her music would be locked up inside of her.

I gave my sister's shoulder a squeeze and said, "It's time for bed. Tomorrow will be a long enough day." As an afterthought, I added, "But tomorrow will be okay, little sister. Really it will."

That night, rain fell—just enough to sprinkle the grass with crystal beads and leave the rose bushes dripping sweetness.

At seven-thirty Sunday morning, I pulled myself out of bed. Minutes before eight o'clock, I stumbled downstairs. For most of the next hour, in between cups of coffee, Irene and I managed to pack five picnic baskets, to answer the doorbell three times, and to squeeze twenty-five lemons for the lemonade.

At nine-thirty, Freddie arrived wearing a bright madras sport shirt and khaki slacks. Within minutes, the picnic baskets and piles of folded tablecloths and jugs of tea and lemonade were carried to the car.

Mama left the house with her apron still on, then saw that she also had on her house slippers, but Freddie walked her back into the house, untied her apron, sat her down, slipped her shoes onto her feet, and tied up the laces. Then he pulled Mama's arm through his and escorted her out the front door.

We were all in the car when we realized Dad was still in the house. When Irene ran up the stairs to call him, Dad came out in his white shirt, his usual suspenders and trousers, with his gray felt fedora on his head. He grumbled most of the way to the car, first about how hot it was going to be, then he got around to mumbling, "Damn Saleem Nicholas. Damn dat man."

"Damn him for what, Dad?" I finally asked.

Irene poked me, leaned over, and whispered in my ear. "Mr. Nicholas beat Dad at checkers at last year's picnic for seven out of eleven games."

Mama sat up front with Freddie. Dad sat on one side in the back and stared out the window. I was in the middle next to Irene. The trunk of Freddie's Pontiac was so loaded, I thought it might scrape against the ground.

Ours was the third car to arrive at Hains Point. Soon afterward, Fords, Studebakers, and Pontiacs piled up behind us into roped-off spaces. By eleven o'clock, the temperature was eighty degrees, but the humidity was low and the waters of the Potomac graced us with a gentle breeze.

Paper was lit with matches, then stuffed under the metal grate of the park's barbecue grills. A group of younger men hauled picnic tables from across the road until a cluster of tables marked off that space for us. Someone set up a badminton net, and the older ladies fussed about its being too close to the tables. By one o'clock, the smell of grilling marinated lamb brought dogs and curious children from other picnic areas to our spot. In our one area, I counted thirty adults, twenty-five children, and at least twenty young adults.

Each time a car drove up, all heads turned to see who had arrived. A whoop would fill the air announcing that a family from Pennsylvania or West Virginia or Maryland's Eastern Shore had appeared.

Within an hour of our arrival, Dad found his checkers partner and, along with four other men, commandeered a picnic table where they sat with elbows on the table, chins resting in the palms of their hands, their backs rounded over the game boards, their eyes narrowing as they calculated moves. The younger children zigzagged around the perimeter in various games of tag. I felt as if it were yesterday that I'd been one of them. Teens clustered together sipping bottles of Coke—girls in one area and boys across the field playing catch or clumped together talking.

Five tables away from where Mama and I were setting out paper dishes and cups, Irene sat on the ground with her back leaning against a tree and a book on her lap. Anthony sat beside her, leaning toward the book. I was too far away to know who was reading to whom.

Just before two o'clock, the games of tag, the laughter, and loud chatter quieted, and people picked up plates and cups and wound their way around tables laden with food: broiled cubes of lamb with onions, peppers, and tomatoes; bowls of *hummus* and the eggplant dip, *babba ghanouj;* stacks of flat bread; jars of freshly pickled beets and turnips; *tabbouleh,* fragrant with mint, lemon juice, and onion; sliced cucumbers in garlic-yogurt sauce and sprinkled with mint; trays of cold stuffed grape leaves dripping with olive oil and tomato; meat pies and spinach-raisin pies; and one bean salad with toasted pita chips on top and another salad loaded with red onions and mint.

The noise of the crowd became a murmur as we snaked our way around the tables, choosing what to eat and debating about which foods needed to be taken now because later there might be nothing left. In groups, we found our way to benches, to lawn chairs that had been hauled from the trunks of cars, and to blankets spread out on the lawn. Voices quieted and we ate and ate and ate. Then ladies began to fan themselves, men stretched out on blankets, young adult couples walked along the railing that separated us from the Potomac's waters. A few mothers called, "Don't go too far!" But no one seemed anxious about the children who strayed.

Mama sat across the table from me, her face perspiring and red. I picked up the fan she'd laid down, leaned forward, and waved it back and forth close to her face. "Tired?" I asked.

She nodded, then reached for an ice cube left in a glass and rubbed it across her forehead, her cheeks, and held it to her wrists.

Thirty minutes later, plates were tossed into garbage cans. Iced tea was passed around. Eight giant coffee percolators were set up on the grates over the red-hot grills. Food was cleared away to make room for platters of nut-filled butter cakes; bowls of rice pudding sprinkled with cinnamon that had been stored in giant coolers; plates of sweet cheese tarts dripping with syrup; trays of crisp, syrupy *bakleh-weh*—some filled with ground pistachios and some with walnuts; pans of nut-sprinkled jellies; and, of course, tins of halvah brought from the Syrian grocery store.

One game of tag started, and chess replaced the checkers games. People milled around the tables, choosing desserts and coffee or iced tea. A second, then third round of Cokes and beer bottles were opened. At the most remote of the tables, where the oldest men sat, a bottle of what I recognized as *arrak*, the foul-tasting homemade liqueur flavored with anise, was passed around.

Freddie organized a softball game, and by three o'clock, most anyone between fourteen and thirty had joined in to play. Freddie was everywhere, coaching, encouraging, and settling disputes. He'd even persuaded Irene to be umpire at first base in spite of the fact that she knew nothing about "out" and "safe." He found a Washington Senators baseball cap to put on her head. And, wonder of wonders! He disengaged Anthony from his grandmother, found him a baseball cap, too, and designated this little kid in a white shirt, short pants, and suspenders to be umpire at third base.

One of the younger girls was pitching when I came to the plate for the second time. I whacked the ball, and before I realized what was happening, I ran past Irene, then past second, then past Anthony at third base. Freddie greeted me with a handshake and a grin when I tagged the sandbag that was home plate.

We finished four innings to loud applause and more pitchers of iced tea and Cokes. Relatives I hadn't talked to in years walked over to chat. Then Freddie came up to offer me a beer. I shook my head and tossed back another gulp of Coke. Several younger cousins came up to thank him for organizing the game.

After he finished his beer, he lay back, lacing his fingers to make a pillow for his head. "The last time I saw you before this summer, I think you were still in grade school."

"Ninth grade, as a matter of fact."

He chuckled. "Boy, time can fly! When I was stationed at Fort Myer, a group of us used to hitch rides into Georgetown. Your mother's cousins were great about feeding us army boys."

"Didn't you go back to Lebanon after the war?"

He nodded. "I was married over there—too briefly to really call it a marriage. After a while, it just seemed right to move on and come back here."

A swell of loud voices edged into our hearing range. A bottle was smashed, followed by another. Women's shrill voices pierced the air.

Anthony appeared, running and out of breath. He grabbed Freddie's hand and tried to pull him to his feet. "Taiteh says you got to come! Now! Nicholas Nader is hitting some man with a beard. He's hitting him pretty hard."

Freddie let Anthony lead him five steps forward, then yanked his hand free. "Wait a minute, kid! You want me to stop a fight between two angry

Syrians? Not me! The ladies'll take care of it! A few of them flashing those deadly stares at their husbands and the fighting will stop. Wait a few seconds and you'll see."

Within two minutes, one after another, the women began stepping in, pulling men away, dabbing male foreheads with dampened cloths. The shouting stopped. The rumbling of the crowd hushed to a murmur.

"But how did you know, Cousin Freddie? How did you know?" Anthony asked.

A smile played around Freddie's mouth. He hitched up his pants then bent down to pick up his empty beer bottle. "I told them to."

"You told them?"

"Sure. Don't you know, if from inside your head, you tell people what they should do and the thing you're telling them to do is really for the best, they'll do it? It's like . . ." He reached up his hand, palm open and grabbed an invisible ball from out of the air, then grinned. "They think they've picked the idea right out of the air themselves. Some day, I'll teach you how it works." He patted Anthony on the shoulder. "Come on. Let's play catch before it's time to head home."

Women started to pack up picnic baskets, fold tablecloths, and dump out scraps of leftover food. I left Freddie and Anthony and joined Mama and Irene who, with several other women, were collecting unused utensils and carrying pots and bowls for rinsing in the water fountains.

When most of the packing-up was done, a distantly related son-in-law gathered everyone together for the usual family photograph. Two picnic tables had to be put together. People stood and sat on benches and on tables. Fathers hoisted small children onto their shoulders. Children bunched together in front of the tables on the grass.

If you look carefully at the developed picture, you can see Band-Aids on wrists and knees marking the scrapes and falls of the afternoon. Several children stuck out tongues and made cross-eyes. But most of the fifty-some who'd gathered were content to obediently say "cheese" when the photographs were snapped.

Shortly before five o'clock, after most good-byes were said, Anthony ran up to Freddie and asked if he could keep his Washington Senators baseball cap.

"Not this time, Anthony. It isn't mine to give."

Anthony's mouth began to sink into the first pout I'd ever seen on his face. "But I'll tell you what . . ." Freddie rested his hands on Anthony's shoulders. "I'll find a hat for you. I promise. You'll have your baseball cap." He patted Anthony on the shoulder, took the cap, and walked away. A few minutes later, Anthony ran back to say there was no more room in Uncle Mike's car. Could Anthony ride to Cousin Usma's with us? Even before Freddie said "yes," Irene took Anthony's hand, said, "There's room next to me," and led Anthony off.

People moved toward cars. Backs were slapped by men who would not see each other for another year. Older women bent to pinch children's cheeks. The grandmothers nodded to each other. *"Ma-a-salameh,"* they said, "God go with you" and "God willing there's another time." Car doors slammed. A few last good-byes were shouted. Engines were started. One car, then another pulled out from its parking space. The Awtooah family left Hains Point for another year.

On the ride home, Irene sat up front with Anthony squeezed in between her and Freddie. By the time we reached M Street, Anthony was asleep with his head on Irene's lap. In the back seat, Mama slept all the way home. On the other side of me, Dad stared out the window. From his impassive face, I couldn't tell if he'd won more games of checkers than he'd lost.

When we got to Prospect Street, Irene walked Anthony down to Cousin Usma's, where his grandmother was waiting. Dad helped Mama out of the car.

Halfway up the front stairs, as if she'd awakened from a trance, Mama yanked her arm away from Dad and snapped at him in Arabic. She walked into the house and started toward the kitchen but Dad followed her, took her elbow, spoke sharply in Arabic, then spoke again more softly. Within minutes, they followed one another down the front hall and climbed the stairs to the second floor.

Freddie and Irene helped bring in the picnic baskets and the bowls and tablecloths that had to be washed and put away for another year.

After we'd unloaded the car and put things approximately where they needed to be, Freddie announced that he was tired enough to fall asleep right there on the spot and had to be getting home.

Although I didn't ask him, I found myself wondering where home was for this distant cousin of mine. When Freddie turned to wave "good-bye" before getting into his car, I was surprised to feel a twinge of sadness about seeing him go.

11

A week after the picnic, Irene walked into my bedroom without her usual knock on my door. "Lottie, he's home! Ralph Alan's home! But he hasn't even been by the courtyard to say 'hello.' He doesn't want to see me! I know that's what it is!"

"But you don't know that! It's just that when he comes home from his uncle's, he has lots of things to do."

"You think so? You really do?"

Several days later, Irene reported that when she and Ralph Alan finally met, Ralph Alan seemed as enthusiastic about seeing her as he always was—"almost like he'd never been away."

"See? He really is glad to see you."

She shrugged. "Maybe, but Ralph Alan always seems happy, and even if he's not, no one would ever know."

I walked up to my sister and put both hands on her shoulders. "Trust, Irene—you have to learn to trust."

The next time Irene met Ralph Alan in the courtyard, she put down her books, then sat on a nearby bench before eventually blurting out, "Ralph Alan, your brother Toby says you're a saint. Are you? Is that what you really are?"

"Toby's only teasing, Irene. Of course I'm not a saint. Saints can't be ordinary people like you and me."

Irene bent down to pick up a maple leaf that had fallen to the ground.

"Do saints get to God's light faster? Is that why they have a halo around their heads?"

"Seems to me saints are saints because they've done really special things and then God gives them the halo as a sign."

"Could you—would you—ever pray to God that Mama could be nicer to me? To have her not yell at me when I spill sugar on the floor?"

"That's not the kind of thing you pray for, Irene. You pray to feel God's love so that you can be happy right here." He patted his chest over his heart. "Happy people just naturally spread God's word about love. You see it all around you in the birds and squirrels and the trees and the sky. Praying's not about asking God to tell people what they ought to do."

When the university bells chimed, Irene picked up her books. "Do people feel God's love in heaven when they die?"

"You don't have to die to feel God's love. You can feel it right here. Just keep praying for God to bring you more of His light."

Irene settled her books in the crook of her arm. "I missed you when you were away. We had a big family picnic, and I was an umpire and it was more fun than I ever thought, but still I missed you. I'm really glad you're back."

That year, for the first time in her life, school was tolerable for Irene. "At least I'm not being made fun of," she told me. "I'm only being ignored."

In her piano lessons, she'd progressed to playing pieces that used both hands at one time, and Mary Ellen reported that Edna was thrilled with the way Irene understood the nuances of a song.

My sister continued to meet with Anthony every Friday. Sometimes she brought books from the library to read to him, but usually Anthony said, "Reading to someone's for babies. I can read by myself!" Sometimes they played "go fish" with a deck of cards they found in a basement junk pile, but usually, Anthony colored in his coloring book while Irene sketched or read.

One evening, out of the blue, Irene asked me if Anthony's father was rich. Anthony's father, Soutine's son-in-law, was someone the family rarely talked about, and I was reluctant to break that rule. "I don't think he's particularly rich," is all that I said.

"But Anthony said that his father lives in a big house and makes lots of money. He showed me a five-dollar bill he said his father sent him last week. Where is Anthony's father anyway?"

"He's out west somewhere, Irene. Soutine and her daughter don't talk about him much."

Irene walked toward my bedroom door then turned back. "It's funny how he only wants to color pictures of planes and cars and boats. I brought him a coloring book with people in it, but he refused to color in it. He said it was 'stupid.' He's cute and he's smart, but sometimes he says things that are a little strange."

In the first week in October, out of the blue, Mary Ellen and Edna asked Mama and me over for "a little chat." They talked about Irene's progress using words like "amazing" and "glorious." Finally, I realized that we'd been invited to "chat" so that they could sound out Mama on whether she would allow Irene to audition for the St. John's Church choir.

When Mama said, "Church? What kind church?" Edna O'Malley rested her hand on Mama's arm. "Irene won't have to become a member of the church, Mrs. Awtooah. She won't have to compromise her beliefs. It would be for her musical training. Lawrence Westlake is one of the finest choir directors I know."

Maybe it was the way Mama swept her gaze away from their faces or the swiftness with which she jutted her chin into the air, but the ladies waited two weeks before mentioning their request again. On a gray October day, they came knocking at Mama's front door after they'd called to be sure I was at home.

"All we want is for you to let her try singing with the choir—let her learn the holiday music. People are coming down with the flu, and one of the girls is having a baby. The sopranos really need her, and the experience will be marvelous."

"We're sure you wouldn't want her to miss out on the training Dr. Westlake can offer," Edna added.

"We'll take her to choir practice and walk her back home."

"Of course she has to audition first," Edna interrupted. "But that's only a formality. We thought maybe, if possible, next Thursday evening she could do that."

"You'll be doing us such a favor!"

The ladies looked at Mama, who certainly didn't understand but managed to smile, which Edna and Mary Ellen must have taken as approval because they gave Mama a round of applause, said "thank you" to both of us, then turned to walk away.

Three days later, Irene followed Edna up the winding stairs that led to the church's music room. The bespectacled Dr. Westlake pushed his glasses up the bridge of his nose and rested his fingers on the keyboard. "So this is the soprano wonder Edna's been telling me about! Well, let's try some scales on 'la' then 'ee.' We'll see how high your voice turns out to be."

Irene looked toward Edna for reassurance, took a breath, and gripped the edge of the piano. Dr. Westlake played scales and arpeggios that led Irene steadily toward high C.

The choir director lifted one hand from the keyboard. "Higher? Think you can do it?"

Irene nodded. He played and she sang until they reached the E above high C.

"Well, I'll be damned," said Dr. Westlake, who sat back and looked more closely at Irene. "Edna, do you think she can sing from this book?" He thumbed through a collection of soprano solos, pointed to a piece, and when Edna nodded her head, he played the piece through once, then started it again, conducting as Irene sang.

When the piece was finished, he sat without moving, closed the book of solos, and turned and looked intently at Irene. Then he motioned to Edna, "Take her into the choir room to pick out a robe—and be sure it's one of the best ones we've got!"

. . .

When word got around in the Syrian community about the Syrian girl who'd been asked to sing in the "Amulcan" church, the cousins clamored to hear Irene sing, and, at Edna's suggestion, two small "concerts" were given at Mama's house. The cousins and their friends from the Syrian Ladies' Club sat in rows at the front of Mama's dining room. I made a point of taking the afternoon off from work for both concerts.

Right on time, Mary Ellen bustled into the front parlor. Irene walked in and stood beside her. Mary Ellen flipped through *Fifty Soprano Songs for Intermediates and Beginners* until she said, "This one! Yes, we'll do this one first!"

Irene turned to face the ten or fifteen people seated on an assortment of kitchen and dining-room chairs. Background chattering quieted as Mary Ellen arranged her ample bottom on the piano bench and ran her fingers up and down the keyboard in a practice scale. Irene cleared her throat and rested one hand on the top of the upright piano while Mary Ellen played the opening chords.

As soon as she began to sing, Irene held herself taller. Her face relaxed. To watch her was to know that when she sang, she was in another world.

At these front parlor concerts, my sister sang "Smoke Gets in Your Eyes" or "Jeannie with the Light Brown Hair," words and sentiments Mama's guests certainly didn't understand, and yet, as the women sat crowded together with arms folded across their chests, some leaned forward to listen more intently and several nodded their heads in rhythm to the songs. Occasionally a foot bobbed up and down keeping time. They applauded and "ooo'd" and "ahh'd" after each song, and when the thirty-minute concert was over, the cousins and their friends crowded around Irene, chattering and patting her arm until Irene backed out of the parlor and retreated to the quiet of her room.

I thought my sister was marvelous at that first concert, but I hadn't an idea of what was still to come.

At the second concert, Irene followed a program of songs similar to those she'd sung before until the last song—when Mary Ellen began playing notes that were familiar to me, notes I associated with Christmas but not Christmas alone. Later I found out that the piece was known as Gounod's "Ave Maria."

The song started gently, something that reminded me of a baby being rocked in a cradle. When Irene's voice joined in, her voice was a velvet ribbon moving in and around the notes. Right from the beginning of the song, her eyes were closed. She seemed to be saying "thank you" to something much, much larger than herself or the people in Mama's living room.

Her voice moved higher as the song went on—up and up a little at a time. I don't know much about that kind of music or about church, but as she sang higher notes, I felt as if, like a minister raising up a chalice, my sister was offering up her voice to be blessed. Higher and higher she sang, and yet I knew her voice was rolling toward notes that were higher still.

The women did not nod or tap their feet this time. For the most part, they sat with their hands in their laps, the faces turned up toward Irene.

As Irene moved toward the final high note, she opened her eyes as if she were eager to give her voice to the universe, and from the shining power of that high note, I was certain the universe would applaud.

As the song gently descended to its quiet end, I saw peace in my sister's face—a glowing, grateful peace.

When Mary Ellen stopped playing, no one moved. Slowly, women brought their handkerchiefs to their eyes. No one talked, no one stood up to leave.

What do you say in the presence of such beauty? Even those who had never experienced that kind of singing before sensed that they'd been blessed by unexpected grace.

After what seemed like an eternity but was probably fifteen seconds, Irene bowed her head to the audience as if she were thanking them for listening to her, then she walked up the stairs to her room.

At both recitals, Mama sat in the far corner, her eyes trained on Irene's face, but it seemed to me her concentration rested on some distant place.

Near the end of the second "concert," I saw Dad slip through the front door and stand by the arch of the hallway entrance to the parlor, his arms folded, his eyes trained on his daughter as she sang. He must have left the store in his afternoon helper's care.

The next day, when I asked Irene what Dad said to her later, her eyes widened, "You mean Dad heard me? He was there? I wonder why he didn't say something."

"All those women, probably. I'm sure he felt uncomfortable." I tried to sound casual, but I thought it was terrible that Dad didn't take more of an interest in the recent opportunities offered to Irene. Irene didn't seem angry at all.

On the Tuesday after Thanksgiving, Mama called me at work, "Dey say Sunday Irene sing in Amulcan church. Next-door lady say we got to go."

The following Sunday was unusually warm for the end of November. Still, Mama wore her one good coat—black wool with a fur-trimmed collar that clumped together as if an animal had been drowned for its fur. Mama's gray hair was pulled back and up under the black helmet-shaped hat of the style that she and her cousins tended to wear.

We walked to the church in silence. Mama stopped every once in a while to catch her breath. She'd pull out a napkin to dab her forehead—stopping so often that finally I had to pull her by the arm. "We're almost late. If we're going, we've got to go."

We slipped into the church, and when I started to lead Mama toward the middle of the church, she yanked me in the direction of a pew at the back. We sat and waited while Mama sniffed, then sniffed again. She leaned over to me. "No smell," she said. I knew that for her, a church without incense and icons was not a real church at all.

When the procession started, we stood, and my mother crossed herself as the cross was carried by. White-haired men walked by us, one or two younger men, thin women, short and round women, but no one as tall as Irene, who brushed by us with her hymn book open as she sang, her shining eyes focused toward the altar. With her hair secured in back with a tortoise-shell barrette, she looked almost like the other neighborhood ladies except for the intense expression on her face.

I don't remember much about the service. I kept waiting for the part on the program that said, "Anthem Solo by Irene Awtooah." When it came, the organ sounded rolling chords. The choir stood and began the anthem. Within the space of a lightning flash, Irene's voice cut high and clear through the other voices, soaring like a bell over mountains. She was in her element. Again, I was amazed at the solid, self-assured sound of her voice.

As soon as the service was over, Mama grabbed my hand and pulled me to the side door of the church. Outside, people gathered, shaking hands and talking—the congregation mingling with blue-robed choir members.

A bespectacled, balding man in a choir robe, whom I assumed was Dr. Westlake, swooped like a giant bird alighting on the group, took my sister's hand, then kissed her on the cheek. Someone stepped forward to take a photograph. Women clustered together in front of the camera, and in the middle of the group smiled my sister, her eyes sparkling with happiness.

Mama yanked at my sleeve, then tugged on my arm and pointed to the stairs leading to the street.

"Mama, don't you want to wait for Irene to talk to her? To tell her how wonderful she was?" But Mama was already headed down the stairs. On the street, she turned, looked up at me, and cleared her throat. "Irene sing good."

That was the first time I'd ever heard Mama compliment one of her children. When I caught up with Mama, she let me link my arm through hers and this time didn't pull away.

On the Monday after she sang in church, Irene left school early in order to find Ralph Alan. "I sang a solo in church yesterday! And Mama and Lottie came to hear me. Afterwards, everyone said how good I was!"

"Sure you were good. Why would you think it would be any other way?"

"And Dr. Westlake thanked Edna and Mary Ellen for discovering me. Can you imagine? And Mary Ellen's going to give me an extra piano lesson on Thursday afternoons."

"Doesn't surprise me a bit."

Irene walked over to the concrete slab on which he'd written her name. "And they might plan a recital later in the spring!"

She crouched and brushed away enough leaves to see the "I" and the "R," then stood up. "And they're talking about maybe sending me to a special summer camp for gifted music students—in Baltimore! For gifted students! Me! Gifted! They're saying that about me!"

"That's great, Irene. Really, it's what you deserve."

She walked over to the bench and sat down. Frown lines gathered on her forehead. "The only thing is, I get scared about the good things. When good things happen, something always comes along to take them away."

"But you don't have to think like that."

"I do, though. Really I do! I'm usually the one who does something stupid to make the good thing go away." She gathered her books, walked toward the tunnel entrance, then stopped. "That's the worst part of all. I just have to wait and wait until the bad thing happens—thinking about it and worrying so I can't go to sleep at night."

"And does the bad thing always happen?"

Irene paused then nodded, adding quietly, "Pretty much—yes, it always does."

That night, my sister came into my room and described her conversation with Ralph Alan. The sleeves of her sweater were pulled down to her wrists, and from the look on her face I guessed that fresh scabs and scratch marks lined the underside of her arms.

"Ralph Alan couldn't even say to me, 'Bad things won't happen.' He only said they don't have to happen. Why didn't he tell me not to worry at all? Why couldn't he be absolutely sure?"

Since I had no answer to her question, I snuck my arm around her shoulder. "It's tough to be so worried how things are going to turn out. I worry, too, sometimes, but usually, the worrying turns out not to be necessary. If you think about it, I'm sure you'll see that's true."

I wished there was something more positive I could've said, but I couldn't think of any words that could have soothed my sister's absolute mistrust of good things or that would, even in a little way, have eased her basic fear.

12

Every year, on the day after Thanksgiving, Mama's awful march toward Christmas began. She scrubbed, polished, dusted, and washed. She banged from bedroom to basement, from front to back porch, cleaning house like a bull let out of its pen.

She rolled out pastry leaves for *bakleh-weh,* her back bent low as she tested each leaf for thinness. She sat for hours shelling and picking walnuts and pecans, her fingers like the needles of a sewing machine as they dipped up and down. She whipped butter, flour, and sugar into the creamy batter that produced her famous butter cookies, her arms swelling like rocks from beneath the rolled-up sleeves of her cotton housedress.

Even during this time of year, members of the Syrian Ladies' Club arrived for unannounced visits—usually minutes after a chicken pie had burned or when a dish had just shattered upon the floor or when a headache had kept Mama from cleaning the day before. Still, Mama forced herself to welcome them with what passed for a smile. What an actress, I used to say to myself.

With the rest of us out of the house, Irene bore the burden of Mama's holiday tension, but this Christmas, she had reprieves. Since Irene's Thanksgiving solo, Mary Ellen began calling to ask Mama if she could "borrow that talented little girl of yours—for just thirty minutes or so."

Although she always had chores for Irene to finish, Mama told Mary Ellen "yes" because displeasing her "Amulcan" neighbor was the last thing in the world she wanted to do. She'd yell upstairs for Irene, saying, "*Hedeh,* dat next-door woman, want you."

When she came into the kitchen to go next door, Irene would find Mama seated at the table, her hand pressed to her forehead.

"Mama, what's wrong? I don't have to go if you don't want me to."

Mama would wave at Irene with the other hand. "Is okay. Go on." And then as an afterthought, she'd snap her fingers. "Get aspirin 'fore you go. Two! And glass water! And headache cloth!"

The first Tuesday in December, a mist like ice crystals hung in the air. Ralph Alan was in the courtyard seated on a bench. Irene told me that he was poking with a twig at a pile of leaves. As soon as Irene put down her books, he spoke without looking up. "Going away again."

"No! You can't!" She clapped her hand over her mouth. "Oh, Ralph Alan, I didn't mean that! Yes, I did! I mean—I shouldn't have said that, should I?"

"It's kind of nice having someone say they don't want me to go away. My uncle had a stroke. They think he's gonna get better, though."

"I'm sorry. I mean—I'm glad about the getting-better part." She walked over to where her name was written in concrete, pulled her coat under her and sat on the brick walkway. "It's just that it gets pretty lonely around here when you keep going away." She traced the "I" in "Irene," then looked up, "Ralph Alan, will we always be friends?"

"I sure hope so. I'll be home from time to time. Besides," Ralph Alan reached down for the stick he'd dropped and drew a large circle in the dirt in front of his feet, "my uncle says everyone is together in God's world no matter where we are."

Ralph Alan closed the circle he was making and poked random penny-sized holes inside of it. "My uncle says the most important part of us, the seed of us he calls it, is really up there in heaven all the time. He says when we get lonely for other people, it's really because we're lonely for a part of ourselves."

The university chimes rang four times. Irene stood up and walked to the other side of the circle that Ralph Alan had made. She picked up a perfectly shaped red maple leaf and laid it on Ralph Alan's lap, then walked over to a bench and collected her books. "How soon will you be leaving?"

"Pretty soon."

"Before Christmas?"

Ralph Alan shook his head. "Not that soon. Uncle's got someone to help him until then."

Late that night, at a time when I thought Irene would have been asleep, she knocked on my door and asked if she could come in.

"You all right? You're looking kind of sad."

She nodded and stood just inside the doorway opening. She looked down at the belt of her robe as she pulled it tighter, hesitated, then pulled the belt tighter again. "Lottie, do you think part of us is already in heaven since that's where we came from anyway? Ralph Alan said it could be that way."

"Well, goodness, Irene. I never thought about that before. I guess it could mean that we return there when we die—kind of like going back home after being away a long time."

Irene remained in the opening of my bedroom door. "Do you think it's possible that we see each other in Heaven after we die?"

"I don't see why not. If God's kingdom is for us all, then I guess after we die, that's where all of us will be."

She thought about my answer, seemed to feel satisfied, then nodded her head and said, "Good night."

Three evenings later, when I came in at eleven from working the night shift, Irene was wide awake and waiting for me in the kitchen. Her eyes were shining with an excitement that I rarely saw. She started talking when I was only halfway through the door.

"Lottie! Listen! There's a chance that they'll let me sing two solos on Christmas Eve! Me! Can you imagine? The woman who sings those solos has come down with the flu, and Dr. Westlake wants me to learn the music just in case!"

"That's wonderful!"

As suddenly as she'd come out with her news, her face became sad. I followed her to the kitchen and noticed redness and scratch marks on the inside of her arm.

In the kitchen, my sister sank into a chair. "I wanted so badly to tell someone about it! I waited and waited for you to come home." Her hand slipped under the sleeve of her sweater.

Irene sat down, then immediately stood up and walked to the kitchen window. "There was no one to tell! I wanted so bad to tell someone, but I couldn't. It shouldn't be allowed that you could live somewhere and have no one around you to talk to who can understand."

She was addressing her words to me, but I had the feeling she was talking to the late night sky.

On the Friday one week before Christmas, the sound of carols floated down to Cousin Usma's basement, where Irene read and Anthony colored. Near the end of that hour, Anthony put down his crayon. "Irene?"

Irene tore a piece of paper out of her notebook and stuck in the page to hold her place. "What?"

"Can Santa Claus make stuff happen when other people can't?"

"Sure he can. Haven't you ever written Santa Claus a letter asking for something for Christmas Day?"

Anthony shook his head. "Taiteh says Santa Claus is for babies." He turned back and resumed his coloring. Two minutes later, he set aside his crayon. "In the letter, the children can ask for whatever they want?"

Irene nodded.

"Is it good if it doesn't cost too much money?"

"It's better if it doesn't."

"And nobody has to know?"

"Santa's the only one who's going to read it."

"Can you send a letter to him from me?"

"Sure. You can write it next time we meet. I'll take it home and mail it so that your grandmother will never know."

"Can I think about it?"

"Sure, but next Friday's two days before Christmas. That'll be your very last chance."

"And you'll bring paper for me to write on? And help me spell the words?"

Irene nodded, then picked up the book she was reading and started toward the stairs.

Anthony collected his crayon box and coloring book and followed her. "And Santa visits every house every year?"

"Yes, Anthony. Every year."

Anthony stopped climbing the stairs and looked up toward Irene. "Cross your heart and hope to die?"

Irene turned enough to look back at Anthony. She nodded. "Cross my heart and hope to die."

The last day of school before the Christmas vacation dawned as icy as if it were January 1. When Irene reached for her plaid wool coat, Mama yanked it out of her hand. "Too cold. Dis coat you wear!" She held out a red coat with a hood that Irene hated. They called her "Riding Hood" whenever she wore the coat to school.

Irene's class had been dismissed from school at 12:30 that day. Wearing her red coat, she was on her way to babysit with Anthony, her thoughts focused on the rehearsal ahead of her that night and the possible announcement that she would be singing the solos on Christmas Eve.

As she turned the last corner to head up Prospect Street, as if he'd come from nowhere, Toby Yanchus was beside her. His hands were jammed into the pockets of his plaid wool jacket and his shoulders were hunched against the cold. "You always daydream when you walk?"

Irene stopped walking long enough to verify that it was Toby Yanchus, then raised her chin and walked faster than before.

Toby's wiry legs kept up with Irene.

Irene tightened her arms around her books.

"Afraid I'll steal those?" Toby continued to follow her. "Okay, ignore me if you want to, but then you won't hear a message I brought from my brother the saint."

Irene had turned partway toward him, hesitated, then held out her hand.

Toby grinned. "Not that kind of message. It's something I gotta say."

Irene started walking again, but more slowly this time.

"Hey, you can't walk and listen, too. Don't you want to know when my brother's going away?"

Irene stopped walking but did not turn around.

"Sometime after Christmas—as soon after Christmas as he can get a ride. He said you should meet him later this afternoon if you can."

Irene took the last few steps to the bottom of Usma's front stairs.

"Well, can you? I'm supposed to let him know."

Irene didn't move.

"Can you?" Toby repeated.

My sister shrugged her shoulders then continued up the stairs.

Just before she reached the cousin's front door, Toby yelled, "Hey! You know what?"

Irene rested her hand on the doorknob but did not turn around.

"You look kinda cute wearing that red coat!"

She yanked the front door open, then slammed it closed.

Anthony made Irene check the kitchen twice to be sure Soutine hadn't come to pick him up before he started on his letter to Santa Claus. He started his letter three times, angled his body away from Irene when he wrote, and occasionally asked how to spell a word.

When he was finished, Anthony folded the paper over before handing the letter across the table to Irene. "Promise you won't tell Taiteh?" He waited for Irene's nod before he released the letter into her hand.

On the outside of the folded rectangle, Irene printed, "To Santa Claus at his home at the North Pole," and told Anthony she would put the letter in "a real envelope" as soon as she got home. She tucked the paper between the pages of her mathematics book, then picked up the rest of her school books and started toward the stairs leading up from the basement.

"When will I know whether Santa Claus got the letter?"

"On Christmas morning."

"Will the present he sends me be waiting under the tree?"

Irene looked back at him. "Yes, Anthony—if he can get the present, it'll be waiting under the tree."

"And Santa Claus comes every single Christmas?"

"I told you he did, didn't I?" She rested her hand on the light switch next to the kitchen door.

"He doesn't ever skip a year?"

Irene flicked the switch off and on. "Come on, Anthony. Mama wants me home soon, and I've got to meet somebody first. I've really got to go."

"You meeting Santa Claus?"

She shook her head. "No, not Santa Claus. Just a really good friend."

In the courtyard, Irene had less than fifteen minutes for Ralph Alan to tell her he'd let her know when he was leaving for his uncle's farm and probably it would be after Christmas Day. Irene had even less time to put down her school books, take the robin's egg Ralph Alan had shellacked to give to her as a gift, say "thank you," and give him the drawing she'd done of his favorite red maple in the courtyard.

Before she could see if Ralph Alan really liked the drawing, she tugged on her gloves, collected her schoolbooks, and hurried out of the courtyard. She didn't see the folded letter that dropped out of her math book and landed on the courtyard pavement.

As soon as Irene arrived home, Mama sent her to the D.G.S. for another five pounds of flour and a box of powdered sugar. Mama asked Irene to rub her shoulders with liniment, to get aspirin, to draw the blinds, and to finish scrubbing the spot on the Christmas tablecloth that Mama's headache had forced her to leave soaking in the basement tub.

Checking the clock to see how much time she had before Mary Ellen came to walk her to choir practice, Irene scrubbed the spot on the tablecloth clean, ironed it, then ironed the napkins for Christmas dinner.

In the kitchen she rubbed silver polish on the sugar bowl, creamer, and the candy dish. She cleaned out the sink and washed down the kitchen table then pulled the pot of rice and lentils from the refrigerator and set it on the stove.

At quarter after five, Irene washed her face, brushed her hair, and pulled on a red velvet headband. At five-thirty, she went next door to Mary Ellen's to run through the solo she'd probably be singing the following night.

"Tomorrow, remember to have her rest her voice, Mrs. Awtooah," Mary Ellen called down the hall to Mama when she came to walk Irene to practice later that evening. Mama stepped from the kitchen to the edge of the hallway and stood with a dish towel in her hand.

"Remind Irene to drink warm liquids and lots of water, too. We can't have our songbird catching any kind of cold." Mary Ellen did not seem to notice that Mama contributed no nod of agreement nor any sign that she was trying to understand.

13

Sometime between the time Irene left for choir practice and the time Dad came home for dinner, Ralph Alan Yanchus knocked on Mama's front door.

I can only imagine the way it must have been: Mama's eyes widening when she saw the broad shoulders and the wheat-colored hair; her mouth tensing as Ralph Alan said, "Hi ya, Mrs. Awtooah!" and held out his hand, which carried Anthony's letter to Santa Claus; Mama stepping back as if she thought Ralph Alan might hit her in the stomach with the letter; Ralph Alan pushing the letter toward Mama as he said, "Your Irene dropped this paper this afternoon. Go on. Take it. Give it to her. I'm sure she's wondering where it is."

Mama must have heard Dad as he climbed the porch stairs after finishing his day at work. She must have dropped the letter onto the seat of the coatrack before hurrying into the kitchen to heat the *judrah* she'd made for his dinner. Dad took off his coat, hung it on the coatrack hook, and headed into the kitchen, unaware that the bottom of his coat hid an envelope containing a letter.

Much later that night, Irene returned from choir practice after Mama and Dad had gone to bed. I assume my sister was humming as she opened the door and took off her gloves, muffler, and coat and was mystified when she noticed the corner of white paper that peeked out from under the bottom of Dad's coat.

She must have listened to be sure Mama and Dad were sleeping, then picked up the letter, saw "To Santa Claus at the North Pole" written on the front, then slid the letter under the sleeve of her cardigan sweater and tip-toed toward her room.

Twenty minutes later, when I returned home from work, my sister ran down the stairs from her bedroom, grabbed my arm, and whispered, "Lottie, I did something terrible!" Before I'd removed my coat, she practically dragged me toward the basement stairs.

We negotiated our way around the junk Mama had stored downstairs and made our way to two high-backed wooden chairs situated near the one working lamp in the basement.

While I unbuttoned my coat, Irene slipped the letter from under the sleeve of her sweater. "I've done something awful, Lottie! I told Anthony he could write a letter to Santa Claus, and now he's asked for something I can't buy—something that can't be bought at all! I never thought it'd turn out like this! Really, I didn't!"

I held out my hand. "Here. Let me read that."

"No. It's better if I read it to you." She smoothed out the paper and took a deep breath. "Dear Santa Claus, I never sent a letter to you before but my friend Irene says you read all the letters and try to bring people the thing they want most. Well, most of all, the very most of all—I want my Daddy to come home at Christmas. I'll do everything right forever and ever. Please, dear Santa Claus, please bring my Daddy home!"

When my heart stopped pounding, I leaned forward and reached for the paper, read it, then read it again. "Bastard!" I said as quietly as I could. And then, because I couldn't help myself, "God damn all of them!"

"Who're you talking about? What's the matter, Lottie? What have I done? What on earth have I done?"

I pressed the letter back into her hand. "Not you, Irene. Lord knows, this has nothing to do with you!"

"I was thinking maybe I can still go to Woolworth's tomorrow and buy Anthony something for Christmas morning—something so he won't feel so sad. Maybe we could even call Anthony's father and get him to say he'll come home soon. We could do that, Lottie, couldn't we?"

"No, Irene, we couldn't." I stood up and turned toward the stairs.

"Why not?"

I climbed one step, then another, then grabbed the railing with both hands and turned back toward Irene. "We cannot, Irene, because—oh, come on! Let's make ourselves comfortable in the kitchen. I've had enough of this basement tonight."

Irene turned off the lamp and started up the stairs behind me. "But we could find out the phone number of Anthony's father and try to call him, couldn't we?"

I shook my head and kept walking into the light of the kitchen. Once Irene joined me, I beckoned her into the far corner by the sink. "No, we couldn't call him. For starters, I don't imagine Anthony's seen his father more than a half a dozen times in his whole life, and none of those times was within the last three years. Come on. Sit down. I'll put the water on. We might as well have something to drink while I tell you what this mess is all about. Mama and Dad are so sound asleep a bomb could go off and they wouldn't hear a thing."

I turned the fire on under the kettle and took out two teacups, milk, and the sugar bowl, then joined Irene at the table.

"Okay. Here's the way it is. Anthony's father is in prison in Illinois. He's been there since two years after Anthony was born. He'd made a fair amount of money running numbers for Vinnie Sacco. Then around the time Anthony was born, he got greedy and started selling insurance policies that didn't exist to little old ladies. Took off in a stolen car. Can you imagine? While Anthony's mother was working her tail off holding down two jobs and dealing with a baby, that bastard was driving around the country, stealing little old ladies blind!"

"But Anthony said that—"

"Do you think for one minute they ever told Anthony even one tiny part of the truth? The kid's probably never even heard his father's complete name. This family and its secrets! That child's living on dreams made of powdered sugar, and one day—oh, Christ! I don't even want to think about it any more!"

"But why didn't they tell him? Why doesn't Anthony know?"

"Because in this family, pretending that unpleasantness doesn't exist is the way we do things. Because Mama and Soutine and all of the cousins haven't a clue that kids pick up whispers and frightened looks." I jumped up to turn off the flame under the kettle before its whistling began, then poured water into the teapot.

I carried the tea to the table and sat down. "Anthony knows damn well that the stories they tell him are lies. Children pick up these things. He probably thinks he did something horrible to make his father go away. Children think that way. Believe me, they do."

I tried to calm myself by sipping my tea. When that didn't work, I marched to the sink and poured the rest of it down the drain. "Know something, Irene? This family's like a bunch of ostriches—sticking their heads in the sand about bad things that happen because they're terrified of what other people will think!"

"Is that why Mama doesn't talk to anyone about Elias and Belle and Rose never coming home to visit?"

I dried my teacup and returned to the table. "That certainly is my guess. I don't understand much Arabic, but I sure know the sound of gossip when I hear these women talk. They're just waiting to point the finger at things in someone else's life that have gone wrong."

"Isn't there something we can do about Anthony? Buy him a present to try to make up for the fact that his father won't be here on Christmas?"

I rested my hand on my sister's arm. "Give me the night and tomorrow. Maybe I can get Anthony's mother to see if she can get his father to call here on Christmas."

"You think you can?"

"I don't know, Irene. But I can try."

Irene sipped her tea in silence until it was nearly midnight. When we parted at Irene's bedroom door, I rested my arm on her shoulder. "We've got twenty-four hours until Christmas Day. Concentrate on your solo tomorrow night at the Christmas Eve service. You're going to be wonderful, I know it. Somehow, this whole thing will turn out all right." I leaned over to kiss my sister on the cheek, and for once she didn't turn away.

.   .   .

It must have seemed like a blessing from heaven when, at quarter to eight the next night, Irene took off her apron, ran upstairs to brush her hair, and put on some of the lipstick I'd let her borrow. She opened the front door to Mary Ellen, who'd come to walk her to church for the Christmas Eve service. Mary Ellen handed Irene a red-and-gold wrapped package.

"Mama! Mama, come look! Mary Ellen brought me a present!"

When Mama finally marched down the hall, her eyes skirted the wrapped package in her daughter's hand and went straight to Irene's face. She lunged forward, grabbed Irene's chin, pulled a napkin out of her pocket, and, with one swipe, wiped the lipstick from her daughter's mouth.

Irene put her present under the tree while Mary Ellen wished Mama "Merry Christmas," to which Mama managed to reply, "Same too."

Mary Ellen put her arm around Irene and pressed her shoulder in a hug. "Your daughter's a special young woman, Mrs. Awtooah—special in many ways. Edna and Dr. Westlake say they haven't heard a voice as natural as hers in a very long time."

While Mary Ellen spoke, Irene looked toward the parlor, then down toward the floor.

"Well, come on, little songbird. Get your coat on and let's head on to church." Mary Ellen turned toward Mama. "Too bad you can't hear her tonight, Mrs. Awtooah. I know you'd be awfully proud."

I don't know what time on Christmas morning Mama received Soutine's phone call.

I don't know how long Mama tried to continue chopping onions for the stuffing we'd be eating later that day or whether she tried to gulp down her fourth cup of coffee or whether she tossed the remaining contents of the coffee pot into the sink.

I do know that whatever simmered inside of Mama erupted into a scream that shot down the hall from the kitchen up to the second floor and made Irene leap out of bed, grab her robe, and slip herself between the corner of her dresser and the wall as she waited for Mama to burst into her room.

For several seconds, Mama stood in the bedroom doorway, her mouth working like a cow chewing its cud. Sandwiched between her bureau and the wall, my sister clutched her stomach while the toes of her bare feet curled against the floor.

Mama's hands pulled at the edges of her apron until her words finally exploded. *"Majnooneh!* You crazy! You know how bad you do?"

Irene could only shake her head.

Mama thundered toward her daughter. She pulled back her hand then slapped Irene across the face. "Who tell you to talk about An-tony fad-der? Who tell you ask for him to come home? Who?"

"No one, Mama. And I didn't—"

Mama jerked her head toward Mary Ellen's house next door. *"Heydeh* lady? Dat sing lady tell you do dat?"

Irene shook her head. "No! I promise!"

Once more, Mama slapped Irene across the face. "Dat crazy boy wit funny hair live down street? Amulcan lady! Now Amulcan boy!"

"Ralph Alan? Are you talking about—?"

Mama grabbed Irene's arm, whirled her around, then shoved her against the wall beside the bedroom door. "Lie! All you talk lie!" Another shove pushed Irene out of her bedroom and toward the stairs.

Mama gave Irene just enough of a push to start her down the stairs, then clomped down after her. "An-tony look for present. He say Irene tell him fad-der come. An-tony sick. His mother sick. Dey all crazy for what you do!" At the bottom of the stairs, Mama grabbed Irene's arm and whirled her around. "All you tink is sing. Sing! Sing! No more sing, you hear? You hear?"

Irene nodded.

"Say! Say you hear!"

"I hear, Mama."

"Now go! Find *heydeh* present!" She shoved Irene toward the Christmas tree.

Irene hesitated.

"Find! You find!"

Irene bent down, looked over the presents, picked up the one tied with a red-and-gold ribbon that Mary Ellen had given her the night before, the one on which the gift tag read, "To Irene. Because you are a light in our lives. From your friends, Mary Ellen and Edna."

By that time, Mama had stormed forward. "You tink you special? Special gotta learn!" She yanked the gift out of Irene's hands and ripped the paper off the package.

"Mama, no!"

But Mama had already torn off the top of the box and pulled out a china cup with tiny gold music notes painted near its rim. She held it up, then charged toward the kitchen.

"No, Mama! Please! No!"

Mama continued forward with the teacup in her hand, its crumpled box sandwiched under her arm.

Irene ran after her but froze when she saw that Mama stood in front of the kitchen sink with the teacup lifted high in the air.

"No, Mama! Please! Mary Ellen and Edna gave that to me! It's special! It's mine!"

But the cup and the saucer had already been hurled into the sink.

Irene ran around the kitchen's round oak table, past Mama, and plunged her hand into the sink. She gathered a few shattered pieces of china before Mama grabbed Irene's arm, pulled her around, and slapped the china pieces out of her hand. She kicked at the china pieces scattered at her daughter's bare feet. "No more sing! No more lesson. No more Amulcan lady in my house!"

Irene backed up against the far corner of the kitchen, her hand twisting her bleeding finger in the folds of her nightgown's skirt. "I didn't mean to hurt Anthony and Soutine and—"

Just as Mama pulled her hand back to hit Irene again, the front hall door banged shut, shooting a stream of cold air down the front hall. Mama stopped for a second to look back, then raised her arm again. Before she could let loose with another slap, Dad strode into the kitchen and grabbed Mama's arm, his calloused fingers a brown rope around Mama's wrist.

Mama tried to pull her arm away, but when she looked up into the face of her husband, his eyes were fierce with determination. For several seconds they stood in silence. When Mama's shoulders finally rounded forward in defeat, Dad dropped Mama's arm.

His gaze settled on the wild eyes of his daughter's face, the mess of her hair, her bloodied hand twisting itself in the skirt of her nightgown. He pointed to her bleeding hand. "Wash," he said, inclining his head toward the hall leading upstairs.

Irene shot a frightened look toward Mama. Dad took Mama's hand, walked Mama into the pantry, stepped back, and lifted his hand as if he were telling a dog to "stay." He waited for his silent instruction to be obeyed, then walked back to Irene, took her hand, and led her to the front hall, where he motioned for her to go upstairs. "Wash. Five hour company come."

Irene stood without moving, her frightened eyes darting up toward his face and then away.

"Is okay," Dad said quietly.

Irene lifted up first one foot then the other as she walked down the front hall, her bare feet slapping against the linoleum floor.

Never, as far as I know, had anything like that happened in our family before. The house was Mama's domain. The children, small or grown, were Mama's domain. But not that day. Not on that awful Christmas Day.

Two hours later, I came home after a shortened shift at work. Dad knocked on my bedroom door. He held a tray with tea and toast and a boiled egg. "Irene need you." He told me as much as he knew about what happened, then nodded toward Irene's room. "You take." He shoved the tray toward me. "See Irene is okay. Stay wit Irene. Tell her is okay."

He waited while I knocked. There was no response. He inclined his head toward the closed door, signaling that I should go in anyway.

I turned the handle and stepped inside my sister's room. She was seated on the edge of the bed, her arms held straight down between her knees like two boards. She did not look up when I walked in.

I put the tray on the dresser. "Dad brought this up for you."

When my sister raised her head, I saw that her nose was red, her eyes swollen from crying. I walked over and knelt in front of her. She let me lift one arm up from between her knees then the other.

Her eyes remained directed toward the floor. "Soutine called Mama this morning about the letter."

"I know."

"Mama blamed me for messing with family things." She raised her head to look at me. "I didn't mean any harm, Lottie. Honestly, I didn't!"

"Of course you didn't."

"Mama says I've got to stop singing lessons."

"She'll get over it. Wait until she gets through Christmas Day."

Irene turned toward the window. "I've been thinking a lot." In the pause between her words, from downstairs I heard Mama slamming the refrigerator door. "Maybe I should stop singing lessons just like Mama says."

"No, Irene! Mama has nothing to say about this precious gift you've been given. You've got that singing voice for a reason! You are going to use it! About that Mama's got nothing to say!"

Irene shook her head. "Mama's right, you know. I'm growing up. I need to learn more about cooking and other things around the house. She's trying to teach me whatever's right."

From the kitchen below us, a pot clattered to the floor.

"She's trying to teach you what was right for living in the old country when she grew up. But not now. Not today. She does not have the right to keep you from living your life and using that glorious talent you've been given!"

"But she's almost sixty years old. I should stay home more and be a helper to her. What if something happened to her, Lottie? Then it would be all my fault."

I stood up and walked over to the window, my back toward Irene. "Oh, Lord! She's really got her hooks into you, hasn't she?" I tried to compose myself before turning around to face Irene. "Why do you think Rose lives in Pennsylvania and Elias stays in Boston and Belle gets far away from Mama as often as she can? Do you think I want to be living in this house at my age? Two more years, if I'm lucky, and I'll have enough saved to go to secretarial school and put a security deposit on a decent apartment. And then you can bet, I plan to be out of here!"

I walked back to Irene, knelt in front of her, took her hands, and held them between mine. "Listen to me, Irene. Mama's life may not have been a great life—maybe not even a happy life—but giving up your singing, giving up your life to follow what she wants will not make her any happier. You were born to Mama, but she doesn't own you. She can't dictate to you what to do."

I stood up and rested my hands on her shoulders. "You've got a gift in that voice. You've got your life to live. This is not the old country. There is nothing that ties you to this house, this town, or that woman! Please try to understand that! Sweetheart, please try to understand!"

My sister lowered her head and I saw a shudder of hopelessness pass through her shoulders.

I stood up, walked over to her dresser, then walked back with the cup of tea Dad had brought up on the tray. "Come on now. Drink this. Drink it and eat the toast, then wash your face."

I helped her raise the teacup to her lips.

"You were such a happy little child—so full of energy, so full of life!"

"I was?"

"I used to stop by your room and watch you playing in your crib just to brighten up my day." I rested my hand against her cheek, then stepped back. "Come on now. Drink up. Then brush your hair and get dressed in your blue corduroy dress. You look like a princess when you wear that dress. I'll go down and help Mama. Don't say anything more about singing or not singing to her. It'll be all right, I promise. Do you understand?"

She dropped her head in a slow, uncertain nod. "Can you come up and get me when Anthony and Soutine come for Christmas dinner? Can you walk with me so I don't have to go downstairs all alone?"

. . . *14* . . .

At two o'clock, Soutine, followed by Anthony and his mother, walked through Mama's front door. Anthony shuffled like a tired old man. Anthony's mother stuck closer to her son than I'd ever seen her do. Not one of them asked about Irene.

Freddie arrived one hour late with a mousy-looking blonde he introduced as "my friend." I'd expected him to do better than a woman as colorless as this female turned out to be.

At three-thirty, when the family moved into the dining room for dinner, I went upstairs to get Irene, then she and I went straight into the kitchen to carry the steaming bowls of cinnamon-dusted chicken and meatball soup to the table. Irene looked in any direction possible so she wouldn't have to look at Anthony or Soutine, then squeezed in at the table between me and Freddie's friend.

Mama sat at the kitchen end of the dining-room table. Dad sat at the other end. As always, we waited for Dad to lift his soupspoon to his mouth, swallow, then nod before the rest of us began to eat.

The most audible sounds at the start of dinner were the clanging of spoons against china and an occasional "Hmm, this is really good!" All I wanted to do was jump up and yell, "Okay, folks. Let's stop the pretense! What about Anthony's father? What about the lies we've been telling each other about that all along?"

When I heard Dad slurping the last drops of soup from his bowl, I got up to collect the plates. Irene was right behind me. Mama was already in the kitchen with her arm elbow-deep in the cavity of the turkey as she scooped out the stuffing of rice, lamb, pine nuts, and cinnamon that always accompanied our Christmas meal.

Irene and I carried two bowls of stuffing to the table, then brought in gravy, cranberry sauce, the *lubyeh,* the string beans and onions spiced with cinnamon, and my favorite, a baked stew of sweet potatoes, carrots, celery, onions, tomato chunks, and cubes of browned lamb.

As we ate, there were "oohs," and "ahhs," and toasts directed to Mama, who had barely touched what was on her plate. Freddie asked Anthony's mother and me innumerable questions about our jobs. When he explained to his friend that Irene had "a voice that would charm a bird," color flushed Irene's face and she turned away.

Irene barely touched her dinner and spent most of her time trying to avoid looking at Anthony, who was seated directly across the table. When Mama jammed an elbow into my sister's arm and said, *"Killeh!* Eat!," Dad glowered at Mama. After that, Mama didn't say another word.

All the women except Soutine helped clear the table and serve the coffee and the *bakleh-weh* and my favorite, *mahmool,* little cakes stuffed with dates or ground walnuts and liberally dusted with powdered sugar.

After dinner, Mama brought out the figs and nuts and nutcrackers. Dad began cracking pecan shells while we distributed the few presents we'd bought for each other: a manicure set for Anthony's mother; a new apron for Soutine; coloring books and new crayons for Anthony; a tie for Freddie a box of candy I'd quickly wrapped for Freddie's friend; and a Washington Senators baseball cap that Freddie brought for Anthony which, when he opened it, actually produced a smile.

I'd gotten up to collect ribbon and tissue paper, when Freddie walked over to the Christmas tree, bent down, and announced, "Ladies and gents, I do believe there's another present here." I'd forgotten the miniature model of a submarine I'd bought for Anthony at Woolworth's the day before.

Freddie held up the wrapped box containing the submarine. "And it looks like it's for someone right here in this room!" Freddie eyed Anthony. "A-N-T-H-O-N-Y. Anyone here by that name?" His eyes made a sweep around the room. "Any takers?"

Anthony eased his arm from around his mother's waist and nodded.

"Well, then, it looks like Santa Claus left this just for you! Bet it's exactly what you wanted to find this morning under your tree!"

Anthony's mother sent a worried look in Soutine's direction, and I kept thinking that maybe a miracle had happened, that maybe someone had contacted Anthony's father and he managed to send a telegram to his son.

Freddie went through an elaborate presentation procedure, shaking the box and listening to see if it rattled. By the time Anthony started opening the present, it was apparent that his skepticism had been replaced by a thread of hope.

When the submarine emerged, Anthony looked at it, scrambled through the remaining paper in the box, looked again at the wooden model then stared up at Freddie with the saddest eyes I'd even seen. He dropped the submarine and swung around to Freddie. "I hate you! I hate you and your submarine!"

"But, Anthony, I thought—"

I stood up. "Freddie, Anthony wanted more than anything in the world for his father to come home for Christmas or for him to write Anthony or call him on Christmas day! That's what he wanted more than anything else in the world!"

Soutine jumped up, pointing her finger at Irene, who stood between the dining room and the pantry, ready to make a quick escape. "You! It's your fault!"

"Mama, sit down!" Anthony's mother's voice sliced through the air as she grabbed her mother's arm and pulled her into her chair.

For seconds, no one moved. Then Freddie reached for a newspaper and began folding the paper into an admiral's hat. "I'm sorry, Anthony. I didn't know. Maybe next year . . ."

Anthony pulled away from his mother. "No! Not next year! Taiteh told me my daddy did bad things and may never be coming home!"

"Well, Anthony, I'm sure your grandmother didn't—" Freddie put the newspaper sailor hat on his head and walked over to where Soutine and

Margaret sat. He swept off the hat and bowed. "I apologize Auntie Soutine, Cousin Margaret."

He took two small steps toward Anthony. "Most especially, I apologize to you, Master Anthony." Then Freddie got down on one knee in front of Anthony and placed his hand on Anthony's shoulder. "Not having a daddy at home's the toughest thing a little boy can face. I know because—because my daddy left my little brother and me when I was thirteen years old and never came back home."

Anthony eyed Freddie warily. "Never?"

Freddie nodded.

When Anthony looked to his mother for confirmation, she nodded.

"You got to be a tough little guy to grow up without a daddy. Sometimes it may even make you want to cry."

"Taiteh doesn't let me cry. Taiteh says it's only little babies that have to cry."

"Well, your Taiteh's right, except that for the really important stuff sometimes crying's necessary, and missing a daddy can hurt more than anything else in the world, can't it?"

Anthony didn't respond.

Freddie stood up. "That's all I wanted to tell you—that and to say I think you're a very brave little boy." Then Freddie reached out his hand to Anthony. "Want to come out onto the porch with me before you go? We'll take the submarine out there, and I'll show you how it comes up from under the water and where sailors look up to find the North Star so they'll know, wherever they are, which way to go in order to find home." Freddie remained in front of Anthony with his hand held out. "Want to?"

Anthony turned toward his mother, who nodded, then raised his hand to take Freddie's.

"Too cold for nonsense!" barked Soutine, but a "shush" from Anthony's mother quieted her.

Freddie walked Anthony toward the hallway. "I'll put my coat around the little guy to keep him toasty warm."

Fifteen minutes later, the front door opened and Freddie and Anthony came back into the house. Spoons stopped stirring. Dad laid down the nut-cracker. All eyes stared at Freddie, whose arm was around the shoulder of a wide-eyed, red-cheeked, smiling Anthony, who carried the submarine tucked under his arm and had a newspaper sailor hat on his head.

An hour later, as our company left, Anthony walked close to his mother, who rested her hand on his shoulder. Soutine walked more tenta-tively than usual and held tightly onto her shopping bag, which carried left-over turkey and her family's few gifts. Freddie stopped to whisper something into Anthony's ear, then turned to thank me for his tie. He did not hold the hand of his lady friend as they walked out Mama's front door.

It took me forever to fall asleep on Christmas night. I felt as if I'd been swept up in a whirlwind and hadn't yet landed on the ground.

The next day at work, I put my name down on every available shift at Rudy's Restaurant, where I'd been working. I searched through the want ads for some other kind of part-time job—switchboard, babysitting, ticket taker. I'd do anything to save enough for the security on an apartment so I could start that secretarial course and stop living at Mama's house.

It had taken that Christmas to make me see as I'd never seen it before. Living my life at Mama's was not living my life at all.

In the third week of January, on a particularly bitter day when Irene was bundled up with mufflers on top of mufflers, our neighbor Mary Ellen signaled Irene to meet her at the bottom of her porch stairs.

Mary Ellen threaded her arm through Irene's. "Wonderful news! Dr. Westlake got a letter from the president of the Washington Area Choir Directors' Association inviting us to sing at the National Gallery of Art, and they specifically want us to do part of the Bach Cantata with you singing the soprano solo like you did on Christmas Eve. It's the chance of a lifetime for us! Now you'll have to come back to us, Irene!"

Irene shook her head and pulled her arm away. "Mama wouldn't want me to go back to the choir, Mary Ellen. She meant it when she said it was time for me to stop singing. Besides, Christmas seemed to be too much for her this year, and she really needs me around the house. I'm happy for the choir—really I am, but it's not something I can do."

"But this is such a wonderful opportunity for people to hear you sing! Certainly your mother isn't serious about not allowing you to sing anymore!"

Irene tightened her outer muffler around her throat and began to turn away. "Mama really means it, Mary Ellen. I couldn't ask her to change her mind."

"But I could talk to her! She might fuss a little, but so far, she's always agreed."

"I don't think so. Thanks very much for telling me about the choir's performance, but right now I've got to see what Mama needs me to get from the store."

The next week, at lunchtime, I was serving near the front of Rudy's Restaurant when two familiar figures came toward me through the restaurant's revolving door. First, Mary Ellen Twitchell, then Edna O'Malley.

When I took their orders, I wanted to ask what really had brought them into Rudy's, but I decided to wait. A half an hour later, when I brought Mary Ellen's apple pie and tea, she patted a place on the seat beside her. "Can you spare us a few minutes, dear?"

I looked around at the tables I was covering, saw that everything seemed okay, and nodded.

"We're concerned about your sister," Mary Ellen started in. "It might sound a bit harsh, but we think—I certainly don't want to criticize your mother but . . ."

Edna leaned forward. "What Mary Ellen means is that we think it's a crime not to let Irene return to her singing."

Mary Ellen patted my hand. "Well, certainly not a crime. Edna's merely saying that your sister has a chance to sing with the choir at a concert at the National Gallery of Art, and she's afraid to talk to your mother. We thought maybe you could find a way to bring it up. I know your mother has her own ideas about how Irene should spend her time, but this is such a wonderful opportunity for her."

"To put it bluntly," Edna interrupted, "We feel not letting her sing might be harmful to her. Singing is so important to her, and not allowing her to pursue it might eventually take its toll. I'm sure you've seen that glow that comes to her face when she sings."

"Of course I've seen it. I'll always remember the way she looked when she sang the solo at Thanksgiving and her voice filled up every corner of the church."

"Then you do understand!"

Edna clanged her teacup into her saucer and slid out of the booth to stand in front of me so that from my seat, I had to look up into her piercing gray eyes. "Lottie, the issue is simply this: your sister's voice is a gift, and if she doesn't use it, that talent and desire to sing can turn inward on her and hurt her in ways you can't imagine." She reached for her coat but did not put it on.

"Hurt her in what ways?"

Edna turned back and looked into my eyes. "Unused, that talent and her desire to sing could become a destructive force—like energy bottled up with no place to go. A person can't get the kind of fulfillment from singing that Irene gets and not feel some anger at anyone who says she can't have that pleasure anymore." She turned and began buttoning her coat.

"But, Mrs. O'Malley, Irene doesn't seem to be angry at Mama."

Mary Ellen slid to the end of the booth and rested her hand on my arm. "Please think about whether there's anything you can do to encourage Irene to take this opportunity—that's all we ask."

"But Irene wants very much to stay home and help Mama. It's important to her that Mama needs her. Deep down, she really loves Mama. It's almost as if in spite of Mama being the way she is, they depend upon each other."

Edna flashed Mary Ellen a look. "Yes, Lottie. That's something Mary Ellen and I already know."

Eventually, I decided to speak to Mama about Irene's singing at the special performance, but I waited until a weekend afternoon when Irene was shopping and Mama seemed rested and in a good mood. While she embroidered at the kitchen table, I gave Mama the details about the concert and reminded Mama how wonderfully Irene had sung after Thanksgiving and at the "front parlor" concerts. "Irene can develop her voice and still learn the things that are important. I know she wants to help you as much as she can around the house—she's told me that herself."

I stopped talking, leaned forward to admire Mama's needlework, then took a different approach, betting on the fact that for all her bitter talk about the two "Amulcan" women, her fear of antagonizing them would finally win out. "Not letting her sing would show disrespect to the talent she was given and to Edna and Mary Ellen. It would be like closing your door on the Syrian Ladies' Club on the day you know they plan to drop by."

Mama kept her needle going but flashed me a look. She jerked the thread to break it, reached for another color and muttered, "Sing—we see."

Three days later, as I'd suspected she might, Mama agreed.

Mary Ellen and Edna set up practices with Irene to get her voice back into shape and volunteered to walk Irene to and from the church for evening rehearsals.

Irene didn't seem ecstatic about Mama's decision. I imagine she was afraid to put too much hope in this opportunity, but when rehearsals began, my sister was noticeably happier, even though Mama's energy continued to lag and headaches plagued her almost every day.

The week after Irene started rehearsing with the choir, Eloise Yanchus waved to Irene from her front porch. She held an envelope in her hand. "Ralph Alan sent you this note in a letter to me. I think he wants to tell you that he's coming home for a few days. I'm sure he'll give you the details in here. He may not be the best speller in the world, but he can tell you what he needs to say."

"Can I take it home to read?"

"Of course you can, child. He wrote it for you."

Irene folded the envelope, slipped it into her coat pocket, and headed home. Fifteen minutes later, with her winter coat still buttoned up to her neck, Irene closed her bedroom door and turned her back to the door in case Mama should walk in. She read the note once, then again.

That night, when Irene knocked on my door, she was beaming. "Ralph Alan's coming home for a visit the following weekend. He says I should come over to his house and visit—either Saturday or Sunday afternoon. He wrote a note to me and sent it to his mother. He wants me to be sure to stop by."

. . .

The Saturday Irene planned to see Ralph Alan, Mama woke up with a headache. Irene fixed toast and coffee and took it to Mama's bedroom. Mama asked for two aspirin and told Irene to pull down the shade. Irene told Mama she'd go to Sugar's and buy more headache powders and to the D.G.S. for vinegar for Mama's headache cloths and that she might stop off at one of the cousin's for a while.

It took her barely two minutes to cover the three blocks to the Yanchus house. An open-backed truck was parked at the curb. Blankets, sheets, shirts, pants, and shoes tumbled out of open boxes. A nightstand, a desk lamp, an empty magazine rack, and a box of tools stood against the far side of the truck's open back.

Irene stopped walking and stared. She took several deep breaths, then forced herself forward into the Yanchus's front yard. She walked up the porch stairs and rang the doorbell.

An out-of-breath Eloise Yanchus answered the door. "I'm so glad you came. I know Ralph Alan wants to see you before he leaves."

"Leaves?"

"Didn't he tell you? He's come home to take his things because it looks as though he might have to stay with his uncle."

"Stay out there at his uncle's farm?"

Mrs. Yanchus nodded, then flipped back a strand of hair that had fallen in her face. "Things have been so crazy this morning." She stepped back to let Irene into the house then turned and yelled, "Ralph Alan—a visitor!" She turned back to Irene, who stood like a statue at the front door. "Come on inside now, child. Get yourself warm."

A girl's voice called out from the kitchen, "Ma, the toast is burning!"

"Oops! I'd better see what's going on." Ralph Alan's mother turned and scurried down the hall.

From upstairs came the sound of a heavy object being dragged across the floor. "I got it!" A male voice yelled. From behind another upstairs door, the voices of several young girls rose and fell. A bedroom door banged shut. "You get that end! I got this!"

Irene looked toward the top of the stairs, where Ralph Alan and Toby stood with a trunk held between them. "Let's go!" said Toby as he began backing down the stairs. Ralph Alan's eyes were on the steps in front of him until halfway down, when he spotted Irene.

"Hi ya!" he said before he returned his full attention to the trunk and the last remaining stairs. They'd just positioned the trunk in the middle of the downstairs hall when Eloise Yanchus yelled from the kitchen, "Breakfast, you two!" '

Toby gave Irene a hand signal that said "hi" and turned back to Ralph Alan, "Guess we'll fit this baby in later." Toby started toward the kitchen, then swiveled his head around and winked at Irene.

When she was alone with Ralph Alan, Irene stared at him as if she were trying to memorize his face.

He ran his hand over his crew-cut hair and flashed an embarrassed smile. "Hair cut yesterday."

"Can we go out on the porch?"

"Well, sure."

Irene followed Ralph Alan out the front door, walked to the edge of the porch, and looked toward the truck parked in front of the house. "Your mom said you might be staying at the farm."

Ralph Alan nodded. "Uncle's not been doing too well. Have to see how it goes."

"What about your father? Who's going to wheel him down the stairs? Take him to Sugar's to buy an ice cream cone?"

"Toby's been doing it when I'm away, and the others are coming along."

"Toby?"

"He's been a big help to Ma when I'm not around."

Irene turned her back to Ralph Alan and looked toward the street. "You're leaving because of me, aren't you?"

" 'Course I'm not, Irene!"

"I know I talk too much. I promise I can be quiet. I promise I can try!"

"My uncle's sick again—that's all. You got your singing and those nice ladies who teach you. You're going to be in eleventh grade next year, and you'll be learning lots more pretty songs."

"There's a big concert coming up at the end of March. Mama wasn't going to let me sing, but Lottie asked her and she said 'yes.' It'd be nice if you could hear me."

"I'll be coming back to visit. You just let Ma know when you're singing and I sure will try to come."

"Are we going to still be friends even though you're living with your uncle?"

" 'Course we will, Irene. Friends don't stop being friends just because one of them goes away."

The tears that had been threatening swelled into Irene's eyes. "Ralph Alan, do you think that after you die you'll get smaller and smaller—until you feel tinier than the tiniest speck of dust that floats in the air?" She dug her hand into her right coat pocket, then into her left.

"Don't need to think about dying now, Irene. Here ..." He pulled a red-and-white checked handkerchief from his trousers pocket, stepped forward, and flapped it in front of Irene. "Use this. It's never been used—go on."

Irene took the handkerchief and dabbed it on the corners of her eyes, then started to hand it back to Ralph Alan, but he shook his head. "Keep it. Ma bought near a hundred of those when they were on sale."

Just as she crumpled the handkerchief into a ball and stuffed it into her pocket, the front door opened and the girl with blond braids appeared. "Come on, Ralph Alan! It's time to eat!"

"I'm coming."

Irene took a step toward the edge of the porch. "Ralph Alan, do you think there's a place somewhere where people can feel safe and warm and fine?"

"That's what heaven's like, Irene—that's what my uncle says. That's why when you die you keep swimming toward the safe, warm light."

"One time you said that God tells you that everything will be all right. Do you still believe that?"

" 'Course I do. Things will be all right. You've got your singing and those ladies who help with your singing and that choir man who says you got such a beautiful voice. And you said they were talking about you maybe going to a special music school next summer."

"Mama's not about to let me go away."

"Sure she will. Just wait and see."

Irene walked back toward Ralph Alan, opened her mouth as if to speak, then closed it, her mouth pulling in toward one corner as she bit down on the inside of her cheek. "Ralph Alan, can I ask you something?"

He nodded.

"I was wondering if—well—if before you go, maybe you could—just for a few seconds—could you maybe hold my hand?"

"Sure. I can, Irene." He brushed his hand on the leg of his corduroy pants and edged his palm upward and out toward Irene's waiting hand. He wrapped his fingers around her hand and pumped down once in a handshake, then unwrapped his fingers and stepped back.

The front parlor window opened and one of his sisters yelled, "Ma says to come on now, Ralph Alan!"

Ralph Alan nodded to his sister, then walked to the front door. "Take care of yourself, Irene. You hear?"

Irene nodded, then lifted her hand and waved. Her hand remained frozen in that position as Ralph Alan stepped into the house and closed the door.

It was several minutes before Irene turned and started down the stairs. She looked over her shoulder toward the Yanchus house, then walked toward the open-backed truck. She reached out first to touch the nightstand and then the sleeve of a blue-and-red flannel shirt that was hanging out of a box. She'd tucked the sleeve back into the open box when something gleamed up at her from under the bushes near the front of the house. She looked, then walked closer to look again. It was the knife Ralph Alan used for his carving, its two blades folded out and turned toward the ground.

She picked it up, looked behind her, snapped it closed, then cushioned it in her coat pocket on top of Ralph Alan's handkerchief. She lowered her head against the cold and started home.

Mama was still resting when Irene walked into the house after saying "good-bye" to Ralph Alan. She went straight to her room and pulled out the handkerchief and the knife from her coat pocket. She smoothed the handkerchief, folded it, then lifted it to her cheek. She carried both the handkerchief and the knife into her closet and put them in an empty shoe box in the back.

Before the day was over, she'd gone three times into her closet to make sure that the handkerchief and knife were still there.

Mary Ellen told me that at rehearsal that night, Irene's voice had cracked near the end of her solo and tears had slid down her face. "Whatever is bothering her is hurting her pretty bad."

Since Mary Ellen didn't seem overly concerned that whatever was bothering Irene might affect her singing, I decided not to tell her that I feared it might.

. . . *16* . . .

The week after Ralph Alan left and three weeks before the National Gallery Concert, Freddie walked through the door of Rudy's as I was adding potato chips to an order of grilled cheese. He asked me if he could talk with me for a few minutes. I added a slice of tomato to the plate, served it, and motioned to Freddie to join me in one of the booths. "Want a cup of coffee?"

He shook his head, but I walked to the counter and poured myself a cup, black and very hot, then led Freddie to a booth in the back of the restaurant.

He settled into the booth and folded his hands on the table. "I stopped by your mother's house today."

"And?"

"It took her ten minutes to open the door, and when she got there she was out of breath. Have you noticed that kind of thing happening lately?"

"Mama's always out of breath. That's what comes of doing fifteen things at once."

"I think she needs to see a doctor, Lottie."

"Mama hates going to the doctor's."

"So do little kids, but their parents take them when it's important."

"And you want me to take her to the doctor because she was late answering the door?"

"At the picnic last summer, did you notice how tired and red-faced she got? And at Christmas twice she stopped talking in the middle of a sentence—as if she couldn't remember what she was trying to say, and at one point, her spoon just fell out of her hand."

"No, I didn't notice. I'm afraid I had other things on my mind."

"Lottie, I'm not a doctor, but something's going on with Auntie Helena that I don't like."

"Have you talked to Irene? Asked her what she's noticed?"

"Right now your sister's pretty much in a world all her own."

"So there's no one else but me to tell Mama that she should see a doctor? Mama, who hates doctors and hates it when one of her children has a suggestion about what she should do! What about you? She'd go anywhere with you."

"I'm not one of her children, Lottie. Besides, I know you well enough to know you'd hate yourself if something serious was going on with her and you didn't step in to do something about it."

"Don't be so sure." I began to slide out of the booth, but Freddie rested his hand on top of mine. "Wait . . . please . . . just a few minutes. I want to tell you a story—something about family and responsibility and . . . well . . . and guilt."

"I got a job to do here. I don't need a lecture right now."

Freddie let go of my hand. "Not a lecture. A story. It's important to me, Lottie. Will you listen?"

I slid back toward the center of the booth. "Okay. I'll listen."

"There was a boy in Lebanon who had skin the color of weak coffee, and, although not a 'hook' nose, his nose was what everyone expected from an Arab. He worshiped his mother, who truly was a beautiful woman. She had clear, sharp features, hazel eyes, and hair the color of a walnut shell. Then a younger brother was born—a beautiful boy with fair skin and hazel eyes like his mother's. The mother died when the brother was three years old. From that time on, the oldest boy hated his brother, but he smiled and pretended to be nice to his brother even though he often did something bad so the younger brother would get in trouble."

I looked more closely at Freddie—yes, his skin was the color of milk-laced coffee and his nose, though not a "hook" nose, was sharp-edged and long.

"The father of these two boys was very strict—even more so after his beautiful wife died. When the oldest boy was twelve, the father became ill with a high fever. He'd never really been well since his wife's death. There was no penicillin in the villages then. Two months later, the father died, and a cousin in America said he'd take the boys to his home in Pennsylvania."

"The older boy is you, isn't it, Freddie? This is a story about you."

He flicked his eyes away from my face and began drawing lines on a napkin with the prongs of a fork. "The boy wanted to go to America so badly—where there were people of all different kinds and maybe it wouldn't matter if his skin . . ." he looked up at me, ". . . if my skin was dark and my nose not so handsome. I was aware that my brother had lost thirty pounds and was thirsty all the time. I tried to blame it on all that had been going on with Dad being sick and dying and leaving us alone. I bought our passage and boarded the boat and pretended my brother's illness would go away."

"But it didn't, did it?"

Freddie shook his head. "I told myself that in America, the 'magic country,' everything would be fine. But he had diabetes at a time when few doctors where I came from knew anything about insulin. A month after we got here, my brother went into a coma and died." Freddie laid down the fork. "He was a wonderful person, Lottie, and my not paying attention to his illness cost him his life."

"And you think the same kind of thing might be going to happen here with Mama?"

"Not the diabetes part. I'm more concerned about something like a stroke."

"Doesn't a stroke mean not being able to do things for yourself—having to be washed and dressed and fed?"

He shook his head. "It may be something else entirely—that's for a doctor to find out. I remember an uncle in Lebanon going through something like that, and it turned out to be a series of little strokes. It may not even be that at all, but it's important to get her checked out."

"Okay. You win. I'll see what I can do about an appointment with the doctor." I slid out of the booth. "But if I come on too strong about it, it's the last thing in the world Mama will ever do."

For the first time since he'd come into the restaurant, Freddie smiled. "Then I guess you'll have to threaten her with calling me."

When I returned to the booth, Freddie had his head back and eyes closed when I spoke. "Next Tuesday. The doctor can see her at eleven o'clock."

When Freddie's eyes opened, his face showed noticeable relief. "You want me to be there when you tell her about the appointment?"

"Probably not, but it's nice to know I've got help if I need it. I really mean that. Thanks."

I decided not to tell Irene about the doctor's appointment until the last minute, which turned out to be the Monday night before we were to go.

When I stopped by her room before I went to work, my sister was bent over her drawing pad with colored pencils scattered around her on the floor. I stuck my head inside the door. "I'm taking Mama to the doctor's tomorrow morning, but I'm working at seven and won't be home until ten. I need you to be sure she doesn't decide to go to the store or to visit someone. It's so early, she probably won't, but still, I need you to make sure."

Irene nodded but continued to lean into her drawing.

"Irene? I'm taking Mama to the doctor's because of her headaches—and because of a few other things that Freddie thought we should have checked out, and I need you to be sure she doesn't go out to the store. Did you hear me, Irene?"

Finally, my sister looked up.

"Will you keep an eye on Mama tomorrow morning? Will you?" After my sister managed to nod, I slipped out of her room.

Three hours after leaving the house to take Mama to the doctor's, I phoned Dad at the store and told him to meet us in the hospital, where the doctor had insisted Mama be taken for tests.

Apparently, Irene didn't hear Dad when he came home later that afternoon—much earlier than he ever came home from working at the store. He started up the stairs, called to Irene, continued up the stairs, then knocked on her bedroom door and, when she didn't answer, he stepped into her room.

Later Dad told me that Irene was seated on the edge of her bed, looking out toward the gray sky of that dreary afternoon. Dad motioned for her to follow him out of the bedroom.

In the kitchen, he filled the kettle with water, lit the burner, and when the water had boiled, adjusted the flame. He hunted for cookies, laid them on a plate on the table, and continued to do something he rarely did—poured tea for himself and Irene. He poured some of his tea into the saucer, drank from the saucer, then sat back in his chair. "Lottie call. Doctor send Mama to hospital."

When Irene didn't react, he repeated. "Mama in hospital for some-ting wrong inside head. Lottie tell you?"

Irene stopped drinking her tea. "Lottie didn't say anything about going to the hospital. She said they were taking Mama to the doctor's— that was all. Why didn't Lottie tell me? What's wrong with Mama?"

"Doctor say Mama need hospital man. Man say Mama stay one night—two, tree. Dey test. Dey look to see."

Irene pushed her cup and saucer away. "Tests? What kind of tests? What's wrong with Mama? You have to tell me what's wrong!"

"Some-ting wit Mama blood. Want to see why she drop tings, why she fall." He pulled out a pack of Camels, his box of matches, and struck a match on the sole of his shoe.

"When did Mama fall?"

"Day before. In doctor office, too."

Irene pushed back her chair and stood up. "If Mama's in the hospital, I've got to be with her! She needs me! She always needs me when she's not feeling well!"

Dad took Irene's hand and pulled her back into her seat. "Doctor man say Mama need quiet."

"But I have to be with her! She'll get worse if I'm not there—I know she will!" Once more, she pushed back her chair. "Mama's sick because I spent so much time with Edna and Mary Ellen before Christmas. It's because I didn't learn to cook and make dinner like she wanted me to!"

Dad tapped the side of his forehead. "Man say some-ting break inside here. Got no-ting to do wit you or me."

"How long does she have to stay there?"

"One night, maybe two. No one really say."

"But Mama's never been away from home for a night! She'll never be able to sleep!" Irene bolted from the table and started toward the front hall. "I've got to go there! I've got to be with her! It's the only way she's going to get well!"

Dad moved quickly, took her hand, and guided her back to her chair. "We stay here. We do what doctor man say."

Irene stared at the top of the table. One hand rose toward her arm then dropped into her lap. Her eyes remained glued to a spot on the table in front of her.

Dad got up and shuffled toward the living room with his newspaper folded under his arm. By the time he was in the living room, Irene had jumped up and run down the hall. She started up the stairs, clutching her stomach. "I think . . . I think . . . I'm going to be sick!"

. . . *17* . . .

For the next three nights, while Mama was in the hospital, Irene cried herself to sleep.

Four days later, Mama came home. The doctor confirmed that she'd had a series of tiny strokes followed by a slightly larger one, but he predicted that within a year, if she followed his instructions, she'd almost be good as new.

Her speech slurred ever so slightly—apparently I hadn't been paying close attention before. Occasionally, objects dropped from her hand, and because this was unpredictable, she had to be careful about carrying things. We got someone in to spend eight hours a day with Mama, but even with the outside help, Irene sat beside Mama for hours at a time, humming to her and holding her hand. Often, she sang Mama to sleep.

Every day, Irene changed Mama's sheets, washed them, put them through the wringer, and hung them out to dry. The next day she ironed them until the sheets were satin-smooth. When Mama woke up in the morning and when she woke up after her naps during the day, Irene was seated in a chair right next to Mama's bed.

School officials called the house to inquire about the days Irene had been absent. When the assistant principal visited one afternoon, he found that the only person home who understood about school and attendance was Irene. Realizing the situation, he backed out of the doorway. "Maybe . . . maybe you could try coming to school in the morning for a week . . . and see how that goes." He didn't wait for a reply.

Irene tried going to school two weeks after Mama came home, but she came home before lunch and didn't return to school for a month.

When visitors stopped by, Irene greeted them, took their coats and hats, ushered them upstairs to Mama's bedroom, then warned them not to tire Mama out. Irene served tea and cakes, carrying plates and cups to and from the kitchen on a tray I'd brought home from Rudy's.

Members of the Syrian Ladies' Club took turns bringing food. When Soutine stopped by, she ordered Irene to rest, but within an hour, Irene would return to Mama's room.

Several times Mary Ellen and Edna called to see how Mama was doing. As far as I know, no one mentioned the concert at the National Gallery of Art.

Freddie turned out to be a welcome contribution to our family in the days after Mama's stroke. He visited often and spoke Arabic with Mama. He knew to put lots of sugar in her tea. He talked to Mama about places in the old country she hadn't seen since she was a child. Occasionally, tears rose to Mama's eyes, showing a vulnerability that I had never seen. Freddie was unflaggingly cheerful with Mama as he encouraged her to exercise her arm. On several occasions, he actually got Mama to smile.

Dad began to stay longer at the store, and when he was home, he shuffled around the house smoking cigarettes and drinking coffee as if he felt lost in the house without Mama's being up and around.

On a Sunday afternoon in early March, Freddie got Dad to play checkers, and when I saw Dad "take" Freddie's last checker on the board, Freddie looked toward me and winked. Clearly, he'd allowed Dad to win.

I poured Freddie a cup of coffee after Dad went into the living room. "That was amazing. You made my father smile."

"What are you talking about?"

"You let him win."

"I didn't let him win." Freddie raised his voice and pitched it toward the entrance to the living room. "Your father's good at the game. He took every move fair and square."

I don't know what prompted me to do it, but I placed my hand over Freddie's, leaned forward, and rested my lips against Freddie's cheek.

When I sat back, Freddie pushed his chair away and cleared his throat. "That certainly was a surprise. I don't often get affectionate gestures from relatives of mine."

"We're hardly relatives—fourth cousins maybe, and nobody knows that for sure. Don't tell me you don't get flattery from all your women."

He finished his coffee and took his cup to the sink, then turned and threw me a puzzled look. "I'm not sure what 'all my women' is supposed to mean, but it definitely doesn't apply."

I walked him to the front door and watched him as he walked toward his car. Before he got in, he looked up in my direction, which pleased me in an unexpected way. I waved to him and smiled.

In the first week of April, Mary Ellen walked into her yard when Irene was hanging out the wash. "Is your mother doing better now?"

"Better, but still walking with a cane."

"Mary Ellen and I would love to give you lessons again, and Dr. Westlake's dying to have you back in the choir. Everyone misses you, Irene."

Irene looked toward the ground, where her toe poked at the first sprouting of a tulip that peeked out from Mama's garden.

"I'm sure you miss singing, too. And you were doing so unbelievably well!"

"I'm all right, Mary Ellen. Please don't worry about me."

"How about if I pay a little visit to your mother—just sit with her a few minutes—kind of ease the idea to her of your coming next door once in a while to get back into your piano playing and to sing."

"I don't think so."

"But surely she won't mind if you come over a half an hour at a time." She rested her hand on top of Irene's. "I miss hearing your voice, but most of all, I miss you. I like having you around."

Irene looked up with puzzled, guarded eyes. "But you don't really know me."

"Nonsense, my dear. I know enough to understand you're sensitive and talented and very quick to learn." Mary Ellen patted Irene's hand. "Please think about what I just said."

"Mama still needs me, Mary Ellen, and I don't want to do anything to make her sick again."

"My goodness, sweetheart! You didn't make her sick! Now get that idea right out of your mind. I'm sure your mother understands the gift you have in your singing voice. She certainly wouldn't want that talent to sit there and go to waste."

During the rest of April, and into early May, whenever Mary Ellen saw Irene, she would say, "Are you ready to try singing yet?" or "Do you think I can call your mother and ask?" and Irene would answer, "Not yet, Mary Ellen. I'd really better wait."

After Freddie had been visiting off and on for more than a month, he began picking me up from work whenever his job brought him to the neighborhood where Rudy's Restaurant was located.

On a night near the end of April, on our way home, he asked me if, on the way, we could drop by his apartment so he could retrieve a phone number and make a quick call. With other men, I would've immediately started calculating what this could possibly mean, but with Freddie, I said, "Of course."

His place was a one-bedroom apartment about five miles up Wisconsin Avenue from Mama's.

The apartment was what I would've expected from a bachelor who seemed to spend very little time at home. Mismatched kitchen table and chairs. A couch covered in navy-blue corduroy with arms that showed faded patches of gray.

The only clue to Freddie's taste and personality were three hammered-brass vases and two brass trays lined up on the floor against a bare wall and an intricately carved wooden folding screen, which I walked up to right away.

"Like it?"

Whatever was or was not clean in the apartment, this piece had been oiled and polished with loving care.

"It came from my grandmother. I brought it back with me from the old country last time. Sometimes I sit in front of it and drink coffee and try to remember what it was like when I was a child back there."

"What was it like?"

He picked up a vase and turned it like a jeweler admiring a newly purchased gem. "My grandmother's house felt like you could live there forever—'comfortable' is what I mean. I spent a lot of time with her after my brother was born. Whenever I had a tantrum, she seemed to know I needed special attention. My father went into rages over what he called my angry ways."

"You? Angry? I can't imagine!"

He nodded. "There were times when I let anger do plenty of harm in my life." He put the vase back in place. "It's getting late. Do you want coffee?"

"I hadn't thought about coffee, but if you want some, that's okay. Is that what you asked me in here for?"

His eyes narrowed as he studied my face, then slowly shook his head. "I honestly don't know what I asked you in here for. For the first time in my experience with women, I honestly don't know."

During April and May, Irene got away with attending school an average of a half a day a week. If she was to be tested on something she attended class just enough to "squeak by," as she put it. She was up before seven o'clock to prepare Mama's breakfast. She would eat her toast and tea as Mama ate whatever Irene had prepared. When the helper arrived, Irene straightened up the house, ironed Dad's shirts, washed clothes and ran them through the ringer, and grocery shopped. She seemed to be getting thinner by the day.

Whenever Mary Ellen saw Irene and urged her not to stop singing, Irene nodded her head, said "thank you," then walked away. It was only after Mary Ellen mentioned to Irene that the week before at choir practice

Dr. Westlake had talked at length about Irene's "remarkable vocal agility" that my sister reluctantly agreed to visit Mary Ellen and "see how it goes." For the first time in months, Irene resumed playing simple tunes on the piano—softly, of course, so Mama wouldn't be disturbed.

I was invited to accompany Irene to Mary Ellen's—probably because the women thought that if we both went next door, Irene would be less likely to change her mind. Edna, of course, would be there, too. At the appointed time, on a Saturday near the end of May, Irene and I knocked on Mary Ellen's door.

We were welcomed as if the two women hadn't seen Irene in over a year. We had tea and cookies until Irene said, "I better try singing now. I can't leave Mama alone too long."

The first piece Irene sang after warming up with scales was "I Dream of Jeannie with the Light Brown Hair," which Irene had sung at one of her "front parlor" concerts. It's an old Stephan Foster song that for me instantly evokes the sadness of loss. Irene stood, as usual, next to the piano. Mary Ellen played while Edna smiled encouragingly from a nearby chair.

Irene leaned over Mary Ellen's shoulder for a clearer view of the music and the words. They went through one page and had started on the second when Irene's voice began to quiver, the notes caught inside her throat, and she began to cry.

Mary Ellen stopped playing. Edna jumped up and stepped forward to wrap her arms around Irene. Then Mary Ellen took over, her ample body nestling against Irene's bony frame. Irene clutched at Mary Ellen as if she neither wanted nor intended to let her go. The crying turned into sobs while Mary Ellen held her and Edna patted Irene's back. Both women murmured, "It's all right, dear. We're here. We'll get you back singing again. You just wait and see."

... *18* ...

As the weather grew warmer, Irene started to gather her long hair at the nape of her neck and hold it back with a rubber band. On days when Mama moved more actively around the house, Irene covered the rubber band with a ribbon she tied in a loose, lopsided bow. The day she met Toby in the courtyard was a day of rubber band and no bow.

Ralph Alan's brother was sitting in the exact same spot where Ralph Alan used to stretch out his legs and lean against a tree. Toby was dressed in blue jeans, a white T-shirt, and a windbreaker unzipped almost to his waist, with a cigarette in his mouth. His eyes were closed.

As soon as she spotted Toby, Irene tried to back away, but she stepped on a twig and Toby's eyes snapped open. "Hi ya," he said with a grin that suggested he'd known she was there all along.

Irene shifted her D.G.S. grocery bag to her other arm and turned toward the tunnel entrance.

"Hey! Wait a minute!" He stubbed his cigarette out, then flipped it into the bushes. "I won't bite. I just got back from taking Pop to the doctor's. I'm a new man! I'm 'Toby the helper,' not 'Toby the bad boy' anymore." He moved to one end of a bench and patted the space beside him. "Take a load off your feet and keep me company for a little while."

Irene remained standing with her back to Toby but did not try to make an immediate escape.

Toby pulled a pack of cigarettes from the side pocket of his windbreaker. "I know I used to drink and steal and stuff." He pulled out a pack of matches, lit the cigarette, then exhaled a thin stream of smoke. "But now that Ralph Alan's gone, things've got to be different. I'm the oldest one in the house, so I gotta change."

Irene tightened her arms around the grocery bag, turned, and started toward the tunnel that led to the street.

"Hey, Irene!"

She stopped walking but didn't turn around.

Toby cupped his hands around his mouth and yelled, "Just wanted to say I must've gotten carried away the day I cut off a piece of your dress."

Irene continued down the corridor, her shoes clattering against the brick sidewalk when she came out onto the street.

On a night in the middle of May, when the air was damp and warm, Dad did not get up from the table to retreat to the living room or to the back porch as he usually did. Instead, he asked for more coffee and smoked another cigarette. When Irene was finished with the dishes, Dad patted the place next to him at the table. "Irene. Sit."

He stubbed out his cigarette, folded his hands on the table, coughed, paused, then cleared his throat. "Mama sickness cost. Spend too much dollar now." He coughed again, pulled out his handkerchief, spat into it, then stuffed the handkerchief back into his pocket. He looked away from Irene as he spoke. "Piano—piano got to send back."

The next day, the school called home to say that Irene had thrown up three times. Mama's helper called Dad, then Dad called me.

Two hours later, I was at Mama's. The corner where the piano had stood was shadowed by emptiness. I climbed the stairs and knocked on Irene's bedroom door. She sat on the edge of her bed, staring into space, her arms ramrod straight and pressed between her knees. Her face told me she'd barely slept the night before.

I knelt in front of her and rested my hand on top of her knee. "We'll be able to rent a piano again. In the summer, I'm going to go to business school to learn shorthand and secretary stuff. I'll get a new job—a better job. We'll have more money after that."

Irene said nothing.

"Certainly, you don't want to stop singing?"

When Irene shrugged her shoulders, I forced myself to say, "It'll be all right, Irene. Eventually, everything will be all right."

"That's what Ralph Alan says."

"And you believe him, don't you?"

"Not really." She pulled her arms from between her knees. The fingernails of one hand began to scratch her other arm. "Remember the time you talked to me about being on the stage in a long dress singing with an orchestra?"

I nodded.

"Remember how you said I'd have my hair pulled back and shiny earrings on my ears and people would applaud and they'd want to hear more and more? I try to imagine that now, but I can't. That person on the stage might have been you or Rose or Belle, but certainly not me."

"But you sang those solos in the choir and everyone said how marvelous you were!"

I flinched at the continuing rasp of her fingernails as they scratched the lower part of her arm.

"It's better if I give up singing, Lottie. It's better if I stop pretending." Irene stood up and walked to the bedroom window, where she stared out into the night. "Remember that girl singing the solos at St. John's? That girl who sang in the front parlor?"

I nodded.

"That girl must have been someone I borrowed. That girl never really was me."

One week later, on a rainy, cool night, Dad phoned me at the Hot Shoppe where I picked up extra hours whenever I could. Mama was already in bed when he'd arrived home from work to find Irene, wearing only a light sweater over her cotton dress, aimlessly sweeping a few crumpled leaves from one side of the porch to the other.

"Irene not good. I put her in taxi. Send her to you. Tonight not good Irene be alone."

When Irene walked through the door of the Hot Shoppe, she seemed like a stranger to me. Clearly, she had lost weight. Her thick hair hung past her shoulders in a tangled mass. I settled her into a quiet back booth with a Coke and movie magazines I collected from the other waitresses on the floor.

Through the remaining three hours before we closed, the magazines lay unopened. Irene sat with one hand resting on the glossy cover of a magazine, the other wrapped around her glass of Coke, her mouth frozen inches away from the straw.

I came over to sit with her whenever I could. Mostly, Irene seemed not to notice I was there. Near her wrists, red scratch marks peeked out from the edge of her sweater. Once, I reached over to touch her lower arm. "Sweetheart, whatever it is, you can tell me."

She startled, like a sleeper waking, then wrestled with the sleeve of her sweater to pull it down—but not before I'd clearly seen fresh scabs along her lower arm.

"Did you hurt yourself, Irene? Here, let me see."

She turned away from me. "It's nothing, Lottie—really nothing at all."

During the evening, other waitresses came over, but when they said, "Can I get you anything, honey?" Irene shook her head and looked away.

Near closing, when I came over to sit with her, she turned to me, her eyes watery with tears. "Why do things always have to change, Lottie? Why does everything always have to change?"

I wanted to shake her and say, "Wake up, Irene! Put lipstick on and rouge! Cut your hair! Be happy about your singing! Then the changes will hardly matter at all," but I looked again at her shoulders rounding with defeat, her hand moving toward the straw in her glass of Coke, then back to her arm where it hovered before reaching once more toward the straw. *My sister, dear sister*—I wanted to say—*how did it come to this for you and what will it take to make such unhappiness go away?*

I edged toward the end of the booth then turned back to pat her on the shoulder and said, without any thought about what I meant or what comfort my words could possibly give, "It's hard, isn't it, Irene? Sometimes life really can be hard."

On a night in early June, when my shift finished at seven, Freddie picked me up from work and suggested we drive to Hains Point.

We drove the twenty minutes without an attempt by either of us to make meaningless conversation. Freddie pulled into a place beside the water, and we walked to the railing to look out at the river. Waves slapped against the cement wall below, and a thousand stars seemed to wink above us. We leaned our arms on the railing and looked toward the outlines of small boats that navigated the river.

Freddie gazed down at the water, then turned his back, leaned his arms against the railing, and looked up toward the stars. "On nights like this, my mother used to take me outside to look up at the stars and show me the patterns they made. My mother was beautiful—high cheekbones, slender, hazel eyes, and light brown hair. One of her great-grandfathers was a Phoenician, or that's how the story goes. And her eyes ..."

He turned to look at me. "... Yes, her eyes were almond-shaped like yours. Your eyes seem always to be smiling, though, and I remember her eyes as being sad—almost as if she knew she were going to die before her time. When she died, I was angry at her and my father, but I was most angry at my brother. And then I kept moving, first to America, then back to Lebanon—then back and forth between the two, looking for something—maybe I still am."

"Funny—you searching for your mother while I spent so much time wishing I could run away from my mine. I actually felt grateful that Irene was born because I knew that some of Mama's criticisms would be shifted to her. If Irene hadn't come along, I probably would have run away."

"A rebel?"

I nodded.

"You don't seem that way to me."

"Usually, I put on a front of being tough, but inside I was scared. The Arab thing didn't help—having darker skin than the 'Amulcan' children in school—especially when everyone else seemed to be blond. I could never bring any of my friends home—couldn't take the chance they'd meet a bunch of gray-haired ladies in centuries-old housedresses sitting around Mama's round oak table babbling in Arabic. I tumbled all over myself to be one of the neighborhood girls—doing things I regret."

"Sex?"

"Well, yes, but even then I knew I was doing it for the wrong reasons. Something about it never seemed right."

Freddie leaned back against the railing. "Does this talk make you uncomfortable?"

"Not really."

He turned back toward the water, reached out his hand and rested it on top of mine. "Actually, I don't even know why I'm talking to you this way."

I turned my hand over and let his fingers intertwine with mine. "That's okay. It's fine—really."

That night was the first time Freddie walked me to Mama's front door after he'd driven me home. I made an attempt at a joke—something about thinking I'd left the days of being walked by a date to Mama's door in my distant high school past.

At the door, Freddie took my hands in his, leaned forward, and kissed me. Then he stood back. "I'm not confusing this with high school, Lottie. High school was about playing games, about experiments and testing people out. For me, dear Lottie, this definitely isn't high school anymore."

The next morning, while Mama was still asleep, Irene poured herself tea and sat down while I was reading the Sunday paper. She sipped her tea, put it down, picked it up, then turned the cup around in her hands, and sipped again. "Lottie, can I ask you a question?"

I nodded, expecting a question about money, about Mama's progress, about whether we could get the piano back.

"I couldn't help it last night . . . I didn't plan to see you, but I was in the living room when Freddie walked you to the front door. Lottie . . . is it possible for someone . . . I mean . . . can you tell me what it's like to be kissed?"

I shouldn't have been surprised by her question but I was. If Ralph Alan was her first and only friend and their relationship was merely friendly, then not only had my sister never been kissed, she probably had never been touched lovingly, not even affectionately, in her entire life! How could I have forgotten that being Mama's youngest and most watched-over daughter meant that my sister would not have experienced any physical demonstration of love at all!

At least as a child, I'd had older sisters who held me on their laps, hugged me, bathed me, and dried me when I was little, cuddling their little baby sister as if she were a treasured toy.

Otherwise, there was a sparseness of affection in our family. On special occasions, the cousins pecked each other demurely on the cheek, but I'd never seen a hug or embrace. I'm sure if it were possible to conceive five children without a loving touch between them, that was exactly what Mama and Dad had managed to do.

I put my newspaper aside. "I don't know if I can show you how kissing feels. But I guess I can try." I walked over to where my sister sat, rested my hand against her cheek and brushed my lips ever so lightly against hers.

I stepped back. "It feels different when it's between lovers, of course—particularly, when there's that spark that tells you there's more to come." I sat down again.

"A spark?"

"You'll find out one day, Irene. One day, after you've sung your heart out at a concert and people have applauded and cheered and a man walks up to you with a bouquet of roses and tells you how wonderful he thinks you are and brushes his lips against you—then you'll know what I mean."

My sister lowered her eyes and shook her head. "I don't think so. I don't think that will ever happen to me."

Through spring and into May, as Mama regained her strength, she'd been amazingly pleasant. I began to worry in June when I heard her chopping lamb so that the thud of her knife against the cutting board reverberated through the house. She began to fuss at Dad when he wouldn't take his umbrella when the skies threatened rain. She fussed at me for becoming what she called "skin um bone," although at the most I'd lost only five or six pounds.

For several months, she refrained from fussing at Irene. Then, as if summer's heat gave her energy, Mama started gathering ideas about things Irene should do. Irene had to learn to make *kibbeh* "so everybody say 'good.' " Irene had to learn to crochet and embroider—something neither Belle nor Rose nor I had been forced to learn.

As soon as school let out for the year, three times a week, before the morning temperature rose, Mama sat with Irene on the couch in the kitchen, leaning over Irene's shoulder to point to where her stitches were too long or showed too much empty space. "Must do again" became Mama's refrain.

. . . *20* . . .

As Mama's list of "learning" lessons grew longer, Irene spent more time at night staring out her bedroom window while scratching the lower part of her arms. Every night before she went to bed, she walked into her closet, pulled out Ralph Alan's handkerchief, rested it against her cheek, then picked up his knife and held it in the palm of her hand.

Even when the temperature soared, Irene took every opportunity to run errands for Mama—anything that took her toward the courtyard where she could steal a few minutes to sit alone by the cement plaque Ralph Alan had made for her.

She'd brush the leaves away and stare at her name written in cement until her eyes brimmed with tears. If she had time, she'd find a bench, roll up the long sleeve of her cotton blouse, and rest her hand on the inside of her lower arm. As her eyes drifted closed, her nails would dig into her skin, dragging over and through remaining scabs until her fingertips became wet with blood.

When, finally, blood dampened her fingers, Irene's eyes would open, she'd dab at the blood with napkins she'd tucked into her pocket, pressing until the bleeding stopped, then she'd pat a napkin down onto her arm, roll her sleeve down over it, and button the cuff of her blouse. The process had become a ritual she knew by heart. Then, carrying whatever pots of food or bags of groceries she needed to bring home, like a sleepwalker, she turned and headed home.

. . .

On an afternoon in July, Irene sat on the pavement in the courtyard with her legs drawn close to her body while her fingers traced the letters of her name on the concrete slab. She didn't see Toby when he sauntered in, didn't hear his step when it brought him five feet behind her, but her body froze when he flicked his cigarette into the bushes.

As he walked to where she was seated on the ground, Irene shoveled leaves and dirt over the concrete slab. She made no acknowledgment of the fact that he was there.

"You think I haven't seen that thing in the ground before? I know my brother made that for you, and you're trying telling me you two were only friends?" Toby chuckled as he sat down on a bench across from Irene. "He's been home, you know."

"Home? Ralph Alan's been home?"

"She talks! Amazing!"

"He's really been home?"

"Twice. One night last month and one weekend the month before."

Irene's eyes narrowed as if she were gauging whether or not Toby was telling the truth.

Toby stood up, jammed his hands in the pockets of his jeans. "You don't have to believe me. But he's been home just like I said." He looked down at her and shrugged. "Just thought I'd tell you." With his hands still in his pockets and his shoulders hunched, Toby turned and walked away.

Toby brought Ralph Alan's note to Irene three weeks after school had ended for the year. It's a tribute to my sister's intelligence that she'd managed to squeak by with passing marks.

The day was sickeningly hot and humid, and I imagine that Irene was particularly reluctant to go home. She wandered into the courtyard and didn't notice that Toby had followed her until he sauntered over to the bench where she was sitting. She startled when he snapped his wrist and flapped a piece of paper in front of her face. "For you. From Ralph Alan."

Irene looked at the paper, then at Toby. "For me?"

He flapped the paper in front of her again. "He said to make sure you got it. Go on. Take it."

She reached out her hand then pulled it back.

"Go on! Read it! I can't wait here all day!"

This time, she reached up and snatched the paper out of Toby's hand. She laid it on her lap and ran her hand forward then back over the paper as if she were ironing one of Dad's shirts. The writing was in pencil and a tear ate a hole along the right-hand edge. Toby remained standing in front of her as she bent closer to read.

Irene,

I'm real happy here at Uncle's farm. I hope you're happy too. Also, I'm seeing a real nice girl who lives on the farm down the road. Isn't that good? We're looking to get married soon. Hope you're okay.

Your friend,

Ralph Alan Yanchus.

Irene stared at the paper, then lowered it and read it again. She looked up and looked beyond Toby's shoulder toward the leaves of a dogwood branch behind his head.

Toby jammed his fingers in the front pockets of his blue jeans, rocked back on his heels, and shrugged. "Getting hitched is what people do, you know."

"But he's only been there a few months!"

"More like six."

"You knew about this?"

"I figured. He talks about her every time he comes home."

Irene crumpled the letter. Her mind seemed to drift into a land of its own.

"Hello? Anybody home?"

Irene awakened from her dreamy state and jammed the letter into the pocket of her skirt. Her mouth bunched to the side as she gnawed on her lip. Her eyes filled with tears, and she pulled a paper napkin out of her pocket to wipe her eyes.

Toby nudged a pebble with the toe of his shoe. "Taking this pretty hard, aren't you? For someone who's only a friend, I mean." He sat down on the bench.

Irene turned her body away from him and continued sniffling into the napkin.

She didn't seem to notice Toby as he edged closer to her on the bench. She didn't feel the touch of his knee when it bumped against hers and wasn't aware that he'd taken her hand until he pulled her toward him. More quickly than it seemed possible, he kissed her on the lips.

Immediately, he slid back to the opposite side of the bench and leaned his elbows on his knees. "Just seemed like you should know—that's all. That it can be nice—kissing, being with boys—sex stuff and everything."

For the few minutes until the university chimes announced the hour, Irene sat motionless, resting her fingertips on her lips. When the chimes finally rang, Irene jumped up and ran toward the courtyard entrance, leaving her books and the bag of her belongings from her locker on the ground beside the bench.

Toby grabbed what she'd left behind and ran after her. "I'll carry these home for you."

Irene snatched her books and the paper bag away from him and hurried toward the tunnel entrance fumbling and juggling the load in her arms as she ran.

Toby called after her, "Did you mind that I kissed you, Irene?" But she was already inside the tunnel. She half-walked, half-ran and didn't stop until she'd climbed the stairs to Mama's front porch.

Several weeks after he'd given her Ralph Alan's note about being married, Toby sauntered through the courtyard tunnel as Irene sat with her eyes closed, scratching her lower arm until it bled. The first time he saw her scratching her arm, he had walked away before she knew he was there. The second time, several days later, he apparently did the same. The third time, the squawk of a blue jay made Irene turn her head.

"You! What are you doing here?"

Toby did not walk closer but jammed his hands into the front pockets of his jeans and shrugged. "Just walking by."

"I don't believe you!" Irene slapped a napkin over her arm and stood up while wrestling with the buttons on her cuff.

"Let me help."

She whipped her body around so that her back faced Toby.

"It's not good to hurt yourself like that."

"What do you care?" Her voice betrayed the tears that welled into her eyes.

With the lightest of steps, Toby walked around to face her, bent forward to place his hand under her chin, and kissed her on the lips. He stepped closer and kissed her again, more slowly and demandingly. The second time he kissed her, Irene did not pull away.

My sister's meetings with Toby were short and intense. For someone as starved for affection as she was, I can imagine Irene responded like a hungry child. Twice, I saw her sneak into the house with her face flushed, her hair in disarray.

From the intensity I knew was within her, I can imagine that Irene let him pull her tightly toward his body, that she no longer resisted the pressure of his mouth and tongue, that she didn't protest when, eventually, he slipped his hand underneath her blouse, then unbuttoned her blouse, pushed up her bra, and brought his face toward her breasts. I'm sure that eventually, her own fingers undid the buttons of her blouse while he ran his hands up and down her arms, before pressing her tightly to him. When, eventually, he slipped his hands under the waistband of her underpants, she'd tried to pull away, but his lips hushed her protest, and that ended that.

Apparently, they met twice, sometimes three times a week. As it had been with Ralph Alan, their meetings were never planned, but Irene took every opportunity to stop in the courtyard, not even admitting to herself what drew her there or what terrible emptiness she was trying to fill.

Each time they met, Irene forbade Toby to walk her home, although sometimes he insisted, following several steps behind. On the days he followed her, neither of them noticed the hand that pulled the curtain back from the upstairs bedroom window when Irene turned to wave to Toby. Apparently neither of them noticed that when Toby walked away, the curtain immediately fell closed.

Late one morning, in the fourth week of their meetings, Toby walked Irene to the gate of Mama's front yard as Irene juggled several loaves of bread. He looked around, then leaned forward and kissed her on the lips.

For the fifth time that month, a shadow figure at the upstairs window stepped aside and let the curtain close. It was the first and last time that Toby kissed my sister in front of Mama's house.

This time, Mama didn't yell, didn't hit Irene, didn't yank her by the arm. In spite of the limp left by her stroke, Mama stormed into Irene's bedroom. She lugged two suitcases into my sister's room, opened drawers, banged, grabbed, shoved, and stuffed Irene's clothes into these suitcases and into paper bags, into anything she could find.

Mama slammed the lids of the suitcases closed, walked up to Irene, and for the first and only time that afternoon, swatted Irene across the face. "You not my daughter! Never! Never come to dis house again!" Then Mama swiveled around, tossed Irene a blouse and skirt, and yelled, "Dress! Take taxi. We go."

Soutine's house was the place Mama selected for Irene's punishment. We found out later that for the first afternoon, Irene had essentially been locked up in the heat of an attic room in Soutine's house. It was only after Anthony grew terrified at Irene's crying that his mother told Soutine the door to Irene's room had to be unlocked or she would take Anthony and find another place to live.

When Dad called me at work to let me know that Irene was at Soutine's, I telephoned Freddie until I finally reached him a little after six. He told me to come over as soon as I could get away from work.

By seven o'clock, I was sipping the tea with rosewater he had waiting in a large ceramic teapot. He even provided pastries from the Syrian bakery on the other side of town, but I was too wound up to eat.

Freddie suggested that I go home and see what Mama seemed to be up to—reminding me to be calm with her—assuming I could be. He also suggested that I call Soutine's daughter and ask her if she knew what was going on. He told me to locate Dad and see if he knew anything and if he did, see what he might be planning to do.

When I protested that Dad never interfered with anything having to do with the discipline of Mama's children, Freddie answered, "Even though your father doesn't say much, there's a special look in his eyes when he looks at your sister. Believe me, he cares."

At home, I found Dad standing in the front hall, creasing the brim of his fedora.

"Go visit Irene."

"But, Dad, it's after nine o'clock at night! Did you call to see if it's all right?"

He shook his head. "No need. Irene my daughter. Take taxi. Need to see."

"What caused this, Dad? Did Mama tell you what this punishment is about?"

"Helena say one boy at Christmas give Mama paper for Irene. Different boy walk her home many time. She see."

"I can't imagine that! Did Mama say anything about Ralph Alan Yanchus?"

Dad shrugged. "Helena not say."

When he moved in front of me toward the door, I reached out to touch his arm. "Dad? Irene might not want to see you. She's probably upset and scared."

When he turned his eyes toward me, they looked like amber nuggets buried in wet sand. "Is okay. I see her. Don't have to talk."

Two hours later, after Dad came home, I heard loud talking behind my parents' closed bedroom door. The following afternoon, Irene was delivered to Mama's by a taxi paid for ahead of time by Dad.

The Sunday after Irene came home, Freddie suggested we take her and Anthony for an afternoon trip to Glen Echo, the amusement park where we'd always gone to brighten our spirits and simply to have fun.

Irene joined us reluctantly—more, I believe, because she preferred being with us to staying at home. We picked up Anthony, who burst out of Soutine's house as if he'd been dressed and waiting since six o'clock in the morning—which he nearly had been.

Soutine followed her grandson out onto the porch, where she insisted on going over "rules." No ice cream for Anthony, particularly chocolate. No rides that "go up and down or around." We were forbidden to investigate the Fun House because the mirrors that distorted the way you looked would cause Anthony to have nightmares.

Freddie folded his arms and nodded with a serious look on his face that said, "I wouldn't dream of doing otherwise."

Although in the 1950s Glen Echo was the place for kids in Northwest Washington to have fun, Anthony had only been there once and Irene didn't remember being there at all.

As soon as Freddie let us off at the large stone entrance of the amusement park, Anthony pointed to the top rim of the Ferris wheel that was visible over the entrance wall, then to the airplanes that swung out and spun above us to our right, and to the bumper cars that were quiet right now in their sheltered space on the other side of the entrance. "I want to do that! And that one! And that one, too! Is there a fun house? I want to go to a fun house, too!"

"Only if you promise not to tell your *taiteh*."

Anthony nodded eagerly, sparked into life, I believe, by Freddie's childlike enthusiasm.

Irene had wandered over to the board where entertainment notices were posted with lists of the dance bands that played in the Crystal Ballroom, glossy photos of dance-contest winners, girls in pastel off-the-shoulder dresses with gardenias in their hair, and men in dark suits, their arms draped around the waists of the smiling girls under a banner that read, "Glen Echo's Ballroom Best."

Irene turned to me with a puzzled look. "I don't even think I know how to dance."

"One night I can teach you. You'll be good at it—I can tell."

Freddie strode toward us with a string of green tickets for rides in his hand. "What do people want to do first?"

"Eat!" said Anthony. "And then the Ferris wheel and the bumper cars!"

"Irene?"

When my sister shrugged, I suggested, "How about walking over to the swimming pool? We can watch the show-offs dive."

Irene responded with a half nod–half shrug, which told me that was okay. Freddie signaled to Anthony to come with him. "You two run along, then we'll meet around twelve-thirty to eat. Sound okay?"

Already Anthony was tugging at Freddie's hand. "Cotton candy. Can I have cotton candy first?"

"Ferris wheel first—no cotton candy if we're going to do the Ferris wheel first."

Irene and I spent an hour at the Crystal Pool watching the divers and couples oiling their bodies before stretching out on blankets on the oblong patch of sandy beach beside the pool. I cheered at the jackknife divers and those who did back flips. Irene mainly closed her eyes and turned her face toward the sun.

After lunch, Freddie took Anthony on a boat ride on which he could actually drive the motorboat in "real wet water" as he put it. They stayed on the boat for three extra rides.

I strolled over to the Fun House, where Irene said she didn't want to go. Instead, she rode the merry-go-round five times in a row, then wandered back to the fenced-off pool.

Near three o'clock, when Freddie and Anthony and I came back from riding the Whip, Irene was no longer at the pool.

I looked at Freddie. Freddie looked at me, then promptly took Anthony by the hand. "Anthony and I'll walk through the arcade. Irene might be watching people at the shooting gallery or maybe she's buying candy to take home. You check out the other side of the park and take a look in the ladies' rooms."

I nodded and was on my way, then yelled back. "I'll take a look in the ballroom if I can get in."

It took me almost twenty minutes to locate my sister in an empty ladies' room at the far end of the park. It could've been anyone crying, of course, but when I looked down near the floor under the stalls, I recognized the front of my sister's shoes. "Irene? It's me. It's Lottie. Come on out, sweetie. Let's wash your face and comb your hair. We've got to get going home, and I'm sure you don't want Mama to see you that you've been crying."

I applied lipstick to Irene's mouth, then rubbed a bit of color into her cheeks. Outside, I bought us each a root beer, and we walked toward the main gate while Irene told me what had happened that made her cry.

She'd been sitting on a bench in front of the pool when she saw a group of girls and boys from her high school. A boy she'd never seen before walked over to her, pulled out a pack of cigarettes, and offered her one. When she declined, he lit the cigarette and sat down as close to her as he could get. She edged away but he kept moving closer.

The next thing she knew, he draped his arm around her shoulder and gave her shoulder a squeeze. "Wanna come see what's behind the shed over there?" He nodded toward a wooden structure marked "maintenance." He flicked his cigarette away, stood up, and held out his hand. "Come on. I don't bite." One of the girls off to the side giggled. He turned to the group and winked. In the meantime, Irene slipped off the bench and fled.

"It's something about me, Lottie. I make them think I'm someone they can do things to."

I was afraid to ask the question but I asked it anyway. "Do things like what?"

Irene looked down at the empty soda cup in her hand. "You know. Touching. Kissing."

"What about with Ralph Alan?"

"All we ever did was talk. Other boys—well, mainly they're mean and they make fun of me. Ralph Alan wasn't mean, and Toby wasn't either. Otherwise I wouldn't talk to them. Otherwise, I'd rather be alone."

"And what's this about Toby?" I decided to pretend I'd seen nothing, although, at the time, I had my suspicions. "I didn't even know you spoke to Toby Yanchus."

She stopped walking and poured the last few drops of her soda onto the ground. "Toby started coming to the courtyard after Ralph Alan moved away. He's not too bad." She looked up from the empty soda cup she'd begun to crumple in her hand and spoke with such directness that I knew she was telling the truth. "Kissing and touching is all I did with Toby. I didn't know how lonely I was until he kissed me. Kissing him made me feel as if I'd finally become real."

"And Mama saw you?"

"As far as I know, she only saw Toby walk me home, but I guess she saw us more than once."

"You sure kissing was all you did with Toby? Toby Yanchus is a guy who's been around."

Irene's head shot up, her eyes blazing with more fire than I'd seen from her in quite a while. "You sound just like Mama when you talk like that— like I don't know my own mind—like I'm still a little girl. Only it's worse with you because I don't expect it—not from you—not from you at all!"

"Well, you are sixteen, and Toby's got to be at least eighteen by now. Hormones will have their way."

She walked over to a trash can, shoved her crumpled soda cup into the pile of paper and bottles then whirled back to me. "You know what? I don't want to have hormones if it means people don't trust you anymore!" She turned in the direction of the main entrance gate and walked too fast for me to catch up without running. I decided it was better to let her have a few minutes alone.

On the way home in the car, I sat in the back next to Irene. I closed my eyes, hoping that a nap would blot out the last part of the afternoon, but the sound of my sister's nails moving back and forth along her arm made even a quick nap impossible.

... *22* ...

Right after our trip to Glen Echo, my relationship with Freddie shifted from friendship to something more intimate—something so satisfying it scared me at times. Sex with Freddie was different than it had been with the few other men I'd been with. With Freddie, sex was honest and strong, as if he knew, above all, that life could be all too short and much too painful. It felt to me that, for him, our touching and holding each other, exciting each other and bringing blissful release was a special touch of heaven on earth that he truly wanted to share with me.

I started sneaking back home from Freddie's in the early hours of the morning. On one of those very early mornings, when I rolled over to get out of bed, Freddie tugged gently on my arm and rolled me back to face him. He ran his finger along my cheek. I closed my eyes and relaxed into his gesture for several minutes.

When I opened my eyes, I started to pull away. "It's really time for me to be getting home."

He turned me back to face him. "No. Wait." He took my hands in his. "I've wanted to ask you—does it bother you very much—us being some kind of cousins or whatever relation we are?"

"You mean, how do I feel about us being such distant cousins we don't even know where the connection is? Why should it bother me?"

He pulled one hand away from mine and raised it to my forehead, resting it there—like a blessing.

My eyes drifted closed to savor that loveliness. "Do you know that what we have right now is wonderful? It's the first time I've been in a relationship for more than a month that I'm not starting to feel used."

He kissed my fingers. "Does that mean what we have right now is good enough for you to consider marrying me one day?"

I didn't even have to think. I nodded and smiled.

Then, before I knew what was happening, he rolled out of bed, and, without a stitch of clothing on, raised his hands above his head, snapped his fingers, stomped his foot, and propelled himself around in a bearlike pirouette. "She will!! She will! Lottie said she will be my wife!"

After I applauded his dance, he dove back into bed and wrapped his arms around me, then kissed me on the tip of my nose. "You're incredible, Lottie Awtooah—my cousin with the funny name. Incredible!" He looked up toward the ceiling. "Did you hear that, God? One day, Lottie will become the mother of my children and my wife!"

I giggled. "In that order?"

"In whatever order you like—as long as the whole process doesn't take too long."

In September, Irene put in an appearance at school for three half-days. She spent more and more time in the courtyard, brushing back the leaves that covered the concrete where Ralph Alan had imprinted her name. On warm afternoons, as leaves drifted down around her, she curled up beside the rectangular slab and slept.

One Saturday, Irene tucked Ralph Alan's knife into the pocket of her corduroy skirt, pulled her sweater down over the pocket so that no one would notice a bulge, then proceeded to the courtyard. She chose a bench as far away from the entrance as she could and, with her back toward the tunnel, tugged off one sleeve of her sweater and rolled up the sleeve of her blouse to her elbow.

She pulled the knife from her skirt pocket and rested it, flat edge down, against her skin. A cardinal chirped from the branch of a maple tree just outside the far courtyard wall. Another answered. Irene closed her eyes and tilted her head up, as if waiting for the duet between the birds to continue. It did not.

With her eyes still closed, she stood the knife on its edge, the narrow end of its blade resting against the inner part of her lower arm. Without looking down, she pulled the knife vertically from an inch above her wrist almost to her elbow. Like a blind person trying to "read" the features of a face, she ran her fingers along the skin where the knife had scraped. Her fingers came away with no wetness, no sign of blood.

She picked up the knife again. This time she looked down as she pressed the knife firmly into the scratch made by the first vertical line. She laid the knife in her lap, closed her eyes, and pressed her hand against the cut until she felt the first warm ooze of blood. With her eyes closed, she pressed harder until the blood edged between her fingers. Moving slowly, as if afraid to disturb her trance, and with eyes still closed, she felt inside her skirt pocket for the napkins she had brought. She pressed them over the cuts and smiled.

Two nights later Irene pulled her desk chair in front of her bedroom window, settled into the chair, and cut a horizontal line intersecting the longer line she'd made on her arm at the courtyard. By the end of that week, a second horizontal line appeared. Each time she cut herself she retraced the earlier pattern and pressed deeply enough to break through the scab that had formed. Near midnight, she washed the cuts and covered them with Band-Aids.

Her sleep after these nights of cutting was long and sound.

One night when Mama was out with the cousins, Dad sat down with me at the kitchen table. "You tink Irene be okay?"

"I haven't heard her crying lately, and as far as I know, she hasn't gotten sick."

He leaned over to strike the wooden match along the side of his shoe. "Tink she maybe wanna go visit Rose in Pennsylvania?"

"I suppose it's possible. Why don't you ask her?"

"I knock on door. She not answer."

"She might've been sleeping. Try again now while Mama's not home."

Dad looked at me, nodded his head, put out his cigarette, then stood up. "Okay. I try."

He climbed the stairs to the second floor. I heard a knock on Irene's door and then the sound of footsteps walking into Irene's room.

Irene sat on the edge of her bed. Dad pulled out her desk chair and turned it to face where she was sitting. He sat down, looked toward his folded hands, then cleared his throat. "Is good you come home."

"Thank you Dad."

Dad reached into his shirt pocket for his pack of cigarettes, pulled a cigarette half-way out then put the cigarette and the pack back into his pocket. "You maybe go visit Rose in Pennsylvania? Good for you to get away."

"Why would I want to go to Pennsylvania?"

"Rose make not so many rule. Maybe you sing some more."

Irene's fingernails scratched at a loose thread on her bedspread. "It's all right here."

"In Pennsylvania you have more tree and sky. Is good to have more tree and sky. In Pennsylvania, maybe you meet someone nice. You marry."

Irene's hand moved toward her lower arm then pulled away. "I don't think so, Dad."

"You no want children?"

Irene did not respond.

Dad stood up and moved the chair back to Irene's desk. "Children good." He lowered one hand into his side pants pocket, pulled out a wallet and took out two five-dollar bills. He folded them in half and handed them to Irene. "What you need, go buy for your self."

"I don't need anything much right now." She looked directly at his face for the first time since he'd entered her room. "But thanks, anyway. You've been good to me—you really have."

Dad reached out to take Irene's hand, placed the folded bills inside it and closed her fingers over the money. "Take. Is yours." He walked through her bedroom door, then turned back. "Be okay, Irene. You try to be okay."

The Syrian Ladies' Club announced that they were giving a picnic in the
backyard of Cousin Usma's house near the end of October. The purpose
was to entertain a group of Lebanese businessmen visiting Washington
who were considering major donations to the church. Before long, the list
of guests had expanded to almost forty people. When the phone calls and
the food preparation started, it was like the Hains Point picnic all over
again.

On a warm, sunny October day, more cars parked along Prospect
Street than I'd ever seen. At Cousin Usma's, under the yellowing leaves of
her grape vine, forty-five people ate and talked and laughed and drank—
iced tea and soda and lemonade as well as an assortment of alcohol in bottles of various colors and sizes.

Eight carefully chosen representatives of the Syrian Ladies' Club and
their husbands attended, along with an unusual collection of young, un-
married Lebanese girls. Although the day was warm, the visiting Lebanese
businessmen were dressed in suits with matching vests that stretched over
rounding bellies. With dark hair carefully combed back and slicked down
with tonic, their eyes wandered over any unattached females who had
reached the age of thirteen.

Irene was assigned the job of passing around trays of cold grape
leaves, freshly baked cheese tarts, meat turnovers, and spinach pies. The
picnic was billed as a "cocktail party," but it looked more like a banquet for
royalty.

Irene wore her dark hair down. Mama had brushed it that morning with one hundred strokes, insisting that Irene soak her hair with warm olive oil before washing it the night before. That afternoon, Irene's thick, wavy hair was almost sleek, held back with a red velvet headband. She wore a yellow long-sleeved dress with an open V-neck that not only put her birthmark in full view but displayed more of her chest than I'd ever seen. It surprised me to realize that my sister, in spite of her thinness, did have a bosom—not Mae West, certainly, not a pin-up on the back of a sailor's locker door, but a gently rounded bosom just right for a girl her age.

Mama spent most of the afternoon in a chair under the maple tree, snapping her fingers for Irene whenever she saw that the men's plates were empty. Every time Irene stood in front of one of the men to offer food, Mama signaled Irene to stand up straight. Several times, one or two of the men came over to Mama and introduced themselves. During these conversations, Mama's dimples took up permanent residence in her cheeks, and large ovals of perspiration spread under the arms of her dress.

For most of the afternoon, mothers paraded their daughters in front of the several groups of men. The females shook hands and giggled while the men stood under the grape arbor mopping their foreheads and cheeks with white handkerchiefs folded into perfect squares.

At four o'clock, after the party had been going for two hours, I grabbed a cheese turnover from Irene's tray, and when I looked up to say "thanks," her eyes had the look of a sparrow trapped in a cage. Half an hour later, Irene complained of a headache and went home. By five o'clock, I'd had enough of the heat and the silly chatter, excused myself, and left.

At home, Irene sat on the top step of the kitchen porch. I joined her, and we sat in silence until I noticed that her left sleeve was unbuttoned, that the scabs along her arm had been reopened and that blood etched its way to her wrist. I stood up and nodded toward her arm. "I'll get something to put over that."

"It's all right, Lottie. You don't have to."

"No. I want to get something—a napkin or a towel."

My sister shrugged and continued the back-and-forth movement of her fingers along her arm.

After I returned, I pressed a cold cloth against her arm. I tried to imagine what went through Irene's mind as she scratched herself so horribly but no thoughts came.

Eventually, Irene turned toward me. "Is it true the men this afternoon were here from Lebanon to pick out wives?"

"Who told you that?"

Irene shrugged. "Some of the other girls. They were picking out the richest men and talking about the gifts they'd get if they married, the kind of houses they'd live in, the number of servants they'd have. Besides, I saw the men looking at me. I know at least two of them whispered about my birthmark because Mama made me wear this silly dress cut so low. So is it true what they said? Is that why all of us were there?"

"Of course it isn't true!"

Irene turned away. "I don't believe you." She returned to rubbing her arm through the cloth—gently, almost lovingly.

I rested my hand on her arm. "I'm going to get some Band-Aids."

When I returned, Irene started talking again as if I'd never left her alone. "And the girls even pointed out the old woman who they said was the matchmaker—a lady in a flowered dress I'd never seen before. They said she decides who's best for whom and works out things like how much money the girl's family would get, whether the man would buy a house here so part of the year his wife can be close to the girl's real home."

"That's ridiculous, Irene. That kind of thing went out with the middle ages. The girls were just trying to get you upset." I applied the Band-Aids then rolled down my sister's sleeve. "There. No one will know."

Irene's right hand reached toward where I'd placed the Band-Aid, then pulled back. Her index finger picked at the cuticle of her thumb instead. When a dot of red appeared at the corner of her nail, she raised her hand to her lips and sucked the blood. Her finger rested against her lips. She lowered her hand and picked at the cuticle again.

Seconds later, she looked up. "Were you ever really, really happy, Lottie?"

"I guess I was pretty happy as a child and for most of my years in school. You've got to remember, I was always one for having a good time. And you?"

"I was happiest those two months I sang in the choir. Walking in the procession on Sundays, singing—having people talk to me like I really mattered—like I really belonged! I don't think I'll ever be that happy again. One morning, Mama'll come into my room and say 'you marry,' and there'll be nothing I can do."

I wanted to tell my sister that nothing like that would ever happen. Instead, I took her hand and tried to smile. "Listen, Irene, if Mama does something like that you can always tell her 'no.' We can even practice that. Isn't that a great idea? We'll practice teaching Irene to say 'no.' "

Irene smiled weakly then stood up. When she brushed the wrinkles out of the skirt of her yellow dress, I pointed to several dots of blood. "You know, peroxide's the best thing for difficult stains."

Irene didn't go to school the following week. Every morning, she stayed in her room until she knew Mama was out of the kitchen, then she'd slip into the kitchen, wrap several slices of bread in a napkin, stuff an apple in her pocket, sip a glass of milk, and tiptoe out the front door.

Every day that week she went to the courtyard, even though for most of that week, a misty drizzle saturated the air. She hoisted an umbrella over her head, dried off a bench with a napkin, and sat. When one arm grew tired from holding the umbrella, she switched. When she got tired of sitting, she walked around the block, then walked around the other way, then walked around again.

On her way home from one of her walks to the courtyard, Irene glimpsed familiar brown corduroy trousers. Ralph Alan was carrying a duffle bag toward a pickup truck parked in front of his mother's house. From the Yanchus front yard, his mother spotted Irene and waved. "Irene! Good to see you! Look who paid us a quick visit home!"

Irene nodded and stared at Ralph Alan, who flashed a smile. "Hi! Irene. Doesn't Ma look swell? Had her appendix out a couple weeks ago, but now she's doing fine. Got to give her another hug and then get a move on." He wrapped his arms around his mother and lifted her off the ground.

Mrs. Yanchus kissed him, then turned to Irene, "Did you hear? He's going to make me a grandmother! My boy is going to become a daddy!"

Ralph Alan heaved the duffle bag into the back of the truck and pulled a tarpaulin over it before he turned toward Irene. "Isn't that great? I'm gonna be a daddy!" He closed the gap between them and patted Irene on the arm. "Hey! Good to see ya! Everything going all right, Irene? Still singing like a canary bird?"

Irene directed her eyes toward the pavement and shook her head.

"What happened?"

"Mama's been sick."

"I heard. Also heard you and Toby were getting to know each other."

Irene's head shot up.

"Toby's a good boy. Army right now is just what he needs." Ralph Alan threw a sheet of canvas over the boxes in the open back of his truck. "Your mama better now?"

Irene shrugged. "She doesn't rest as much as she should."

"I'm sure you're a big help to her—you always were. Hey, I gotta get going. You be sure and take care of yourself now. Stop by and visit Ma some time. She thinks you're a real nice girl." He waved once more to his mother, who stood at the top of the stairs.

Ralph Alan walked around to the driver's side of the truck. "I'll probably be back around Christmas. Probably bring Marilyn—that's my wife. You can meet her. You'd like her." He stepped up into the driver's seat, closed the door, and started the engine.

Even though the university chimes had already announced that it was four o'clock, Irene watched Ralph Alan back out of his parking space, and drive to the first stop sign. She lifted her hand toward the back of the truck and waved until his truck passed out of sight.

... 24 ...

Mama's big announcement came on Sunday morning two days after Ralph Alan told Irene he was going to be a father. Dad had left for his Sunday walk, even though wind and rain whipped branches to the ground and car wheels spun on piles of glistening leaves.

Mama was washing breakfast dishes. Irene sat at the table, sipping the last of her tea. Mama poured more soap powder into her dishpan and spoke without looking at Irene. "On Tuesday come very nice man from picnic to visit. Name—Saleem. You dress nice. Maybe Lottie help you buy. Saleem nice man—very nice man. Come to visit Mama, have tea. Want to see Irene."

Irene put her teacup down and walked to the kitchen window.

"Irene, you hear?"

At the window, Irene rubbed her hand along the sleeve of her blouse, then turned and picked up a dishtowel and began drying the dishes from the drain board.

"Irene?" Mama turned to look at her daughter and waited for Irene's answering nod. As soon as she got it, she went back to washing dishes and chattering about the Syrian Ladies' Club and how Irene would become a member when she reached eighteen and how Louise's daughter, Selma, would be marrying a man from the "old country" next month and that Matilda probably would be, too, and how they both will live in the "old country" but will spend six months out of the year in Washington, too.

When she handed Irene the last dish to dry, the sound of rain splattering on the back porch filled up the silence. Mama held onto the dish and looked directly into Irene's eyes "Saleem say you very nice—say he very much like my girl."

Irene dried the last dish, reached into the closet, put it away, then hung up her dishtowel to dry. She turned toward Mama but spoke with her eyes directed toward the floor. "Do you want me to marry him, Mama? The man who's coming on Thursday?"

Mama wiped her hands on the dish towel. Her face softened. Her lips slipped into a crack of a smile. "Is nice if you marry. You be happy. Saleem very nice."

Irene turned away and pressed her hand on her stomach. "I think I ate too much breakfast, Mama. I'll take the garbage out later. I'm going to lie down in my room a while."

"You got woman ting?"

Irene nodded.

Mama walked to Irene and tapped Irene's stomach lightly. "One day baby, maybe many baby." Then Mama pulled Irene's chin forward and looked into her eyes. A smile spread like melting butter across Mama's face.

A few minutes later, in her room Irene walked to her window and opened it as wide as it would go. A breeze whipped the curtains in front of her, splattering rain into her hair and onto her face. She wiped the wetness with the back of her hand and closed the window.

She walked to her bed, reached out to hold onto the edge of the mattress for support, and lowered herself to her knees. She leaned forward to slip her hand under the sheets, probing near the foot, near the middle, then near the head. When she withdrew her arm from under the mattress, Ralph Alan's knife was in her hand.

She slid her feet noiselessly down the hall. In the bathroom, she closed and locked the door. She put the lid down on the toilet and sat with the knife in her right hand.

"You okay, Irene?" Mama's voice carried up from the bottom of the stairs.

"Better, Mama. I'll be in the bathroom, then I'm going to nap."

She stood behind the door and listened until she heard sounds in the kitchen and eventually the slam of the door to the basement. She walked back to the toilet and pushed up the sleeve of her sweater.

She sat for several minutes with the flat side of the knife blade pressed against the scabs on the inside of her arm. She put the knife down and pushed the sleeve of her sweater nearly to her shoulder. She picked up the knife, closed her eyes, and pressed the knife edge lightly into her skin, scratching but not breaking the skin's surface. Then, in one swipe, she sliced down to her elbow.

Blood seeped from the gash she'd made, washed into the palm of her hand, down her fingers, onto her leg, and onto the floor. Her right hand pressed into the wound as she rocked forward and back, forward and back. Her mouth relaxed. The creases in her forehead began to disappear.

Two hours later, the bathroom was sparkling clean. The wound was covered with gauze, her clothes and shoes, the towel and knife were shoved into the farthest corner of the closet in her room.

Monday was unusually warm for the end of October. Irene tried going to school, but during third-period social studies, she asked to go to the bathroom and never returned. On Tuesday, she took some of the money Dad had given her, and leaving the house with her school books, she hid them in the courtyard and walked to the corner of Wisconsin Avenue and O Street and raised her hand to flag a taxi.

"Where to?" the driver asked without turning his head.

"The lions."

The driver gave her a puzzled look. "What?"

"I have to see the lions at the zoo."

He nodded and signaled for a right turn. Twenty minutes later, he let her out at the entrance to the zoo. It was quarter after three when Irene walked back through the gates of the zoo and hailed a taxi to take her home.

Mama was waiting for Irene at the door. "Where you been?"

Irene shrugged and headed up the stairs. "School. They kept me late at school."

I found out later that Irene made six attempts to reach me by phone at the restaurant that evening. Four times she hung up before the phone rang in the restaurant. Twice, she heard one of the girls answer, "Rudy's" and then hung up.

On Tuesday morning, Irene stood for an hour on a footstool while Mama pinned up the hem of a dress Soutine had given her to wear.

"Don't you think it's too short, Mama?"

Mama took the straight pin out of her mouth and said, "Is fine," then ordered Irene to turn "little bit."

By Wednesday morning, Mama had hand-washed the dress and ironed it and starched its white collar. She had Irene try it on and walk down the front hall stairs. Then she had Irene try on headbands until they found a blue one that made Mama say, "Nice. Plenty nice."

In mid-afternoon, when Irene came up to her room to rest, she found a faded jeweler's box on the top of her bureau. She lifted up the hinged top and saw a gold-trimmed cameo the size of a half-dollar piece. She put down the box and went to the top of the stairs. "Mama? There's some jewelry in a box on my dresser."

Mama walked from the kitchen down the hall, wiping her hands on her apron, then looked up at Irene and nodded. "From my *immeh*. She give me when I marry. You marry soon. Is time you have."

Irene started to walk down the stairs. "Thank you, Mama. That's very nice, but . . ." Mama had already started toward the kitchen and was already halfway down the hall.

That afternoon, Mama was on the phone with Soutine, who arrived an hour later with Anthony, who ran to join Irene as she snapped green beans on the back porch. Even though the kitchen door banged behind him, Irene gave no notice that she heard him.

When Anthony said, "Can I help?" my sister shrugged and handed him the bowl. "Hold that under my hands right there." She grabbed a bean, snapped off its end, then snapped it in two.

Anthony held the bowl exactly as she'd asked. "Did you know Freddie's been calling my Daddy out where he's in jail?"

Irene frowned and continued snapping bean.

"Really he has! Don't you believe me? Mommy's already told me my Daddy's trying to do better. He runs the printing press in prison now. He's going to do that when they let him out." From his position seated at her feet, he looked up at her. "Irene, are you listening to me?"

She nodded. "Closer! I've got to have the bowl closer."

Anthony raised the bowl until it almost touched Irene's hands. "Freddie says we might even go out and visit my daddy—Mommy and me. And when my daddy gets out of prison, he wants to come home or maybe stay out there and we'll come live with him and I've been asking God to make it happen just like you said. He lives way out near the sun—isn't that what you said?"

Irene had already slipped out of her chair, walked to the door of the kitchen, and pulled it open.

"Irene? What's the matter? You left the string beans out here!"

She didn't stop and didn't turn around. She walked through the kitchen and straight upstairs, where she stayed until after dinner.

From eight until nine that night, Mama walked into Irene's room first to inspect the dress for wrinkles, then later to check that Irene's shoes were polished, then again to demand that Irene put down her drawing book and hold out her nails for inspection. Mama bent close. "In morning, you clean again." She walked through the door, then turned and took five steps back into Irene's room. "Use plenty soap."

Irene sat by her window until midnight, her eyes staring into space. Eventually, she put on her nightgown and climbed into bed, but the baritone rattle of Dad's snoring reverberated through the hall making it nearly impossible to sleep. A little after one o'clock, Irene got out of bed. She didn't throw a robe over her flannel nightgown even though the October night was cold.

She walked purposefully down the hall to Mama and Dad's bedroom, stood still, and listened. When she turned the door knob, the door floated open.

Mama slept on the window side of the double bed, one arm flung over her head, her wrist touching Dad's pillow. Nearer to the door, Dad slept on his side. From the outline under the blanket, his knees seemed to bend toward his chest. Mouth open, his body jerked periodically as he snored.

Irene walked toward the window side of the bed and stood looking at Mama. She reached out her hand toward Mama's face, then pulled it back. She stepped closer and reached out her hand again. "Mama?" she whispered. Mama's eyes remained closed. Her head edged toward the arm that was flung above her head. Irene leaned closer. Her words came as more breath than sound, "Mama, please. I'm trying . . . If only you could . . ."

When Mama stirred, Irene jumped back. Mama lay still again and Irene edged sideways with her back to the window. She kept her eyes focused on Mama as she crossed to Dad's side of the bed.

She reached out her hand toward her father's shoulder but immediately pulled it back. She leaned in toward him a second time, but a loud snore that startled him into changing his position made Irene take several steps backward toward the door. She looked toward Mama, then Dad, then Mama again. Then she backed up to the door, pushed the door open, slipped through the door and closed it, then drifted down the hall to her room.

At the window, she looked up toward the near-perfect globe of the moon. She raised her arms toward the sky, then opened them as if to welcome in the moon. In bed a few minutes later, she fixed her eyes on that light until the moon slipped from view. And then she slept.

. . . *25* . . .

The morning the visitor was to come for tea, Irene dragged herself out of bed. Mama fixed a boiled egg, which she insisted that Irene eat, then she said to Irene, "Cousin Usma say come get flowers from her garden. Saleem come at tree in afternoon. You go soon."

At eleven o'clock, Irene headed down the street to collect the chrysanthemums that Cousin Usma had placed in a straw carry-bag for Irene to take home. On her way home, at the courtyard entrance, Irene paused. She looked toward the nearly leafless trees, the piles of brittle brown and yellow leaves, then stepped into the corridor. She shuffled along the walkway and put down the mums near the concrete slab, which only someone who knew of its existence would find. She brushed the leaves aside and traced the letters of her name, then the outline of the bird. She moved her finger back to the "I" and went over each letter again and again.

Two hours after she left home, my sister climbed the stairs to Mama's house. When she reached the porch, the front door flew open and Mama emerged, her eyes blazing. She took two steps onto the porch with her hand pulled back as if to hit her daughter, then she lowered her hand and snatched the bag of wilting flowers. "Upstairs! *Y'allah!* Soon—soon he come! You wan me dress you like baby?"

Half an hour later, Irene came down, dressed in the outfit Mama had finished sewing two nights before. Her shoulders hunched forward as if she were trying to shrink to hide her breasts.

Mama grabbed her by the hair and yanked back Irene's head then she inspected her daughter's face and pointed upstairs. "Go back. Wash face more." She pulled her hand away and gave Irene a shove up the stairs.

Ten minutes later, when my sister came downstairs again, Mama straightened the white organdy collar of Irene's dress and checked her fingernails.

Irene had just poured herself a glass of water when the doorbell rang. Mama crossed herself and yelled to Irene. She looked down at the front of her apron, reached behind her to untie it, then left the apron on. "He here! He here! *Y'allah!*"

When Mama opened the front door, she extended her hand to a dark-skinned middle-aged man of medium height and build. *"Keef-ak!* Welcome to my house!" She stepped back and let her guest pass into the hallway in front of her. He bowed, then handed Mama his hat.

Saleem was dressed in a charcoal gray double-breasted suit. The corner of a white handkerchief peeked out from the pocket of his coat. His hair was slicked back with tonic, but tonic had been unable to tame a double wave that dipped across his forehead.

With both hands holding her guest's hat in front of her, Mama nodded toward Irene. "Dis my daughter, Irene." She smiled a flash of approval. "Irene, dis Saleem."

Their visitor bowed again and smiled showing yellowed teeth. He extended his hand and spoke in Arabic directly to Irene.

Mama stepped forward and interrupted in Arabic, shaking her head and wagging her finger toward Irene. She let out a nervous laugh then nodded toward her daughter, *"Heydeh,* she wanna be Amulcan. You teach her Arabic. You teach her how to be good Syrian girl."

Saleem shifted his feet, squeezed out a nervous smile, and extended his hand to Irene a second time. The fingers that clasped Irene's hand were cold, the palm moist. He bowed again, stepped back, then reached into the back pocket of his trousers, pulled out a handkerchief, and dabbed at his forehead.

Mama led her guest into the living room then nodded to Irene. "Get tea and cake. Is time for tea and cake."

In the kitchen, Irene stood facing the table like a statue. She pivoted toward the stove, then to the refrigerator, then back to the stove, and still she did not reach for the tray, did not turn on the kettle.

From the front parlor came Mama's voice. "Water boil yet?"

"No, Mama." The comment propelled Irene toward the kettle and then to the sink. She filled the kettle and placed it on the stove.

"Irene?"

"Yes, Mama."

"Saleem come to meet you. Come. Get to know Saleem. He say he want to hear you sing." Mama said nothing when Irene failed to respond.

Irene picked up the two plates of cookies that waited on the table and carried them into the front parlor. She walked up to Saleem with the plates, but Mama waved Irene away and hissed, *"La!* No! Tea come first!"

Irene nodded but continued to hold the two plates, as if she hadn't the slightest idea about what to do next. Mama pointed to the coffee table, and Irene leaned forward and put down the plates. As she stood up, she noticed that Saleem's eyes were glued to the birthmark on her neck. When her eyes met his, he turned his head away. Irene switched her attention to the gold ring with a red stone that glimmered from Saleem's little finger. When Mama hissed, *"Skitteh!* Enough of that!" Irene pulled her eyes from the ring and moved into the kitchen.

In the kitchen, the kettle began to whistle, but Irene ignored the sound and walked over to the window. One hand moved across to the other arm. Her fingernails raked. The kettle whistle shot through the air. Mama thundered into the kitchen, turned off the flame, and spun Irene around. Mama's eyes flashed as she nodded her head toward the living room like a goat butting a wall.

After Mama had stormed back to where Saleem sat waiting, Irene turned toward the window and stared toward the few gold leaves that clung to the ends of branches in Mama's back yard.

Again Mama yelled from the living room. This time, Irene shuffled toward the stove, picked up the kettle, put it back on the burner, turned up the flame, then turned back toward the window. Seconds later, the kettle burst into a furious whistle and sputtered boiling water onto the stove.

When Irene ran to turn off the burner, boiling water splashed onto her hand. On her second try, she turned off the flame. She reached for a pot holder, picked up the kettle, then put it down. She stared toward the tray, took one step toward the teapot, then turned again toward the kettle and picked it up. She poured water in each of the cups, put the kettle back on the stove, and picked up the tray.

She took one step, then a second step. The cups rattled in their saucers. She rested the edge of the tray against the table until the cups stopped rattling. As soon as she raised the tray away from the table, the clack of china against china started up again. She looked around, as if to see if there was some other way, took a step, then another, banged her elbow on the wood trim of the pantry that led to the front of the house. The tray slipped from her hands and crashed to the floor.

Faster than Mama could make it into the kitchen through the pantry, Irene had run down the front hall and out the front door.

Thirty minutes after Irene ran out of the house, I received a phone call from Mama. I called Freddie, who said he'd pick me up right away. I telephoned Dad, whose response was immediate. "I take streetcar to Wisconsin and Calvert. Walk home."

"That's a long way, Dad."

"We find Irene."

By five o'clock, Freddie and I arrived at Mama's. When Irene didn't turn up at any of the cousins' or Edna's or Mary Ellen's, Freddie and I walked the neighborhood. Mary Ellen came to help. We went to the D.G.S., Sugar's, even walked over to the high school and to Visitation Convent grounds. Between us, we covered a radius of about fifteen blocks.

Back at Mama's, we sat. The sky had darkened and a chilly November drizzle iced the air. Dad hadn't phoned, and Mama forbade us to call the police.

Around nine o'clock I thought of the courtyard. "Come with me," I said to Freddie. The drizzle had turned into a late October rain.

We'd gone down Mama's front steps and headed east toward the Courtyard Apartments when Freddie poked me with his elbow. "Look."

Ahead of us, outlined by the halo of street lights and front porch lamps, a tall, hunched figure carried someone in his arms. Dad had thought of the courtyard, too.

Freddie ran to Dad and helped stand Irene on her feet. He wrapped his suit jacket around her. They slung one of her arms around each of their shoulders. Her cotton dress was soaked, and mud layered her arms and legs. Dark strings of wet hair splashed around her neck and shoulders.

On the porch, Mama and Mary Ellen waited.

Mama's hand flew to her mouth when she saw Dad and Freddie carrying Irene. Then she ran down the stairs, spewing angry words in Arabic, her hands beating the air. "*Maznooneh!* Crazy!" was the main word I heard. Dad turned his shoulder so she couldn't get to Irene.

With Irene's arms around each of their shoulders, Dad and Freddie continued up the porch steps. At the front door, Freddie asked Irene if she could walk inside by herself. When she nodded, he buttoned his jacket at her neck. At that moment, Mama turned toward Mary Ellen. "You! All trouble start with you!"

That's when Dad pulled Mama by the arm and slapped her across her face. Then Dad nodded to Mary Ellen, who backed away and headed down the stairs.

For what seemed like minutes—after Freddie, Dad, and Irene had gone into the house, Mama stood with her hand pressed against her cheek where Dad had slapped her. Then Freddie came back onto the porch. He walked up to Mama and patted her on the shoulder. "It's all right, Auntie Helena. It's going to be all right." He rested his hand on her shoulder, and as he turned her toward the house, Mama seemed to shrink into the half-circle of his arm.

· · ·

Irene slept for most of the following day. Mary Ellen came with freshly made turkey soup, which Mama did not refuse.

On the second morning, at ten o'clock, Mama bustled into Irene's room. She didn't notice that her daughter's eyes were puffed from crying, nor did she see the lines on Irene's arms that were crusted over with the blood of fresh scabs.

Mama snapped open the curtains and raised the shade. She pushed open the window. "Is good. Fresh air good." Not once did she look toward Irene, who lay face down on her pillow with her eyes tightly closed.

Mama lunged for a pillow that had fallen to the floor and whacked it with her hand, then dropped it beside Irene's head. She moved along the bed, smoothing the spread and blankets, slapping at wrinkles. Then, as if she'd just realized that Irene had not turned over or opened her eyes, Mama sank her fingers into Irene's shoulder. "Is okay! Saleem say it be okay."

Still lying on her stomach, Irene squeezed her eyes more tightly closed and turned her head away.

Mama shook Irene's limp arm. "Irene! You hear what I say?"

With great effort, Irene turned over and looked up at Mama.

"You hear? Is okay! Saleem call. Next week he come visit again. Is good!"

Irene blinked and blinked again.

Mama smiled and nodded. "You get better."

"But, Mama . . ."

"Saleem come visit again soon."

Irene dragged herself into a seated position. With shoulders hunched, she squinted through tear-swollen eyes. "Mama, I . . ."

"He say you probably afraid. He say 'Many good woman afraid.' He like you. Say you seem like nice girl."

Irene squeezed her eyes shut, then opened them and blinked as if to see if she might still be asleep. "Mama?"

"Is good! You see." Mama had moved to the bottom of the bed. She pulled out each corner of the bedspread then tucked it in again, slapping and smoothing as she kept up a stream of words about Saleem, about "the old country," about the marriageable daughters of the women of the Syrian Ladies' Club.

"But, Mama, I don't want—"

Mama's words came faster and louder as she turned her back and dusted the edge of Irene's dresser with the skirt of her apron. "Saleem got two sister. Got house in Beirut. Family live dere too. Saleem make lots money. At church—"

Irene sat up and inched toward the headboard of her bed, her knees drawn up toward her chest. "No, Mama." she whispered. She turned her head from left to right, then again left to right, her forehead wrinkled, her eyes squinting in disbelief.

Mama continued straightening—first the pictures on the wall, then curtains.

Irene's words came in breathy whispers. "Mama. No, Mama. No! Please, no!"

Mama moved from the dresser to the bookcase, picking up first one china piece, then another, dusting its sides, its top, its bottom. "Saleem say you be good wife. He come see you next week for tea."

Irene hugged her knees to her chest and rocked her whole body left and right. She rocked forward and back, then from left to right again until in one convulsive move, she rolled off the bed, thudded to her knees, and plunged her hand under the mattress.

At the sound of Irene's knees hitting the floor, Mama turned, but by then Irene had pulled out the knife and shoved the sleeve of her nightgown toward her shoulder. With the knife in her other hand, she snapped her head toward Mama, who stood dumbfounded by the sight of her daughter and the scabs along her arm. Irene's chin rose defiantly in the air. She turned and raised the knife and brought it down on top of the existing scabs on her lower left arm as if she were hacking at a tangle of vines.

With her palm open, Mama lunged forward, but Irene yanked the knife away. Mama screamed and looked down at the palm of her own hand. For a moment, no blood appeared. Then it trickled. Then it streamed. Mama grabbed the wrist of her bleeding hand and held it up.

On the floor, Irene bent over her arm, her body rounding forward, her hair carpeting the floor.

Mama looked at her daughter, then at her own bleeding wrist, then threw her head back and howled. Within seconds, still holding her wrist with one hand, she hauled herself down the stairs.

Mary Ellen first heard then saw Mama as she ran onto the front porch. By that time, Mary Ellen had climbed the stairs to see for herself. Irene was huddled in the corner, rocking her body, holding her arm, which bled into the skirt of her nightgown.

Mary Ellen backed away and downstairs. With tears choking her voice, she first phoned me and then the police.

. . . *26* . . .

At Georgetown Hospital, they treated Irene's wounds, then admitted her for psychiatric evaluation. Doctors recommended at least a four-month stay at St. Elizabeth's Hospital, Washington's red brick Gothic institution that served the "mentally disturbed." A week before Thanksgiving, my sister was admitted.

We were told that for the first month of Irene's stay at St. Elizabeth's, or Saint E's, as the hospital was known locally, family visits would not be permitted. "Treatment adaptation" was needed during the time it took for patients to adjust.

Mama did not take kindly to the pronouncement that Irene needed to be in a hospital. She fussed and fumed as she chopped lamb or worked cookie dough, muttering about "Doze Amulcan doctor" or "Amulcan don't know what dey do!" Eventually, I understood that American doctors were interfering with something that never would have been interfered with in the "old country"—a mother's God-given right to be with the only child she had left.

Through the Christmas holidays, even though no Christmas celebration was planned, Mama polished and dusted and scrubbed until, abruptly, she would sit at the kitchen table with an untouched cup of tea in front of her, either staring at her hands or out the window toward the gray December sky.

I noticed the return of a tremor in her hand and the twitching of a muscle near the corner of her mouth. When I'd tell her that Soutine or Cousin Usma was on the phone, she would shake her head and turn away with no indication that she'd understood at all. I checked the number of pills left in her bottles to make sure she was taking her medications and reminded myself that I could take her to the doctor's if I became worried about her health.

Dad talked hardly at all during that bleak early winter. He stayed longer at the store, just as he had after Mama had her stroke. Even on bitter January days, his Sunday walks lasted up to three hours in mid-afternoon.

More than once, he stopped partway from the kitchen table to the sink and asked, "When?" I understood exactly what he meant and answered as gently as I could, "Not yet, Dad. The hospital said 'not yet.' "

At work, more than once, I picked up a sandwich, took a step toward a table, then found I was unable to move. Several times I wiped down a table and by the time the table was clean, my eyes had become watery with tears. At the end of the second week of my sister's hospitalization, I signed up for extra hours at both Rudy's and the Hot Shoppe. It was work, not even Freddie's comfort, that I needed most.

"How could she hate herself that much?" I would ask him, and, rather than telling me not to worry or that "hate" was too strong a word, Freddie would put down the newspaper he was reading and sit closer to me with his hand resting on top of mine.

It was during those awful days that I knew that if I were ever to marry, it would be to this often funny, sometimes sad, and always authentic cousin of mine.

I paid my first visit to Irene in the third week of January. Despite Freddie's offer to accompany me, I insisted on visiting my sister alone. I wanted to focus entirely on my reaction to seeing my sister in that place. I needed to walk inside that red brick building alone.

On a prearranged visiting day, I was shown to a room that received its light through oblong windows crisscrossed with black metal bars. "Hospital?" I asked myself as I was ushered into the visiting room. "Prison" was more the way it seemed to me—a prison with a fake solarium look.

Patients were dressed in slippers and robes—so many people smoking in one room that I wondered if, through the haze, I would recognize my sister at all. Irene stood by a window staring into the space beyond, and I recognized her instantly by the tumble of her dark hair and her willowy form.

When I said, "Hello, Irene," she responded with, "Hello, Lottie." When I asked, "How are you feeling?" she answered with a shrug. I positioned myself not too close and not too far away. For about ten minutes, I waited—shifting my weight from foot to foot while Irene stared out the window as if she'd forgotten I was there. Did she hate me because I'd allowed her to be taken to that place?

Eventually, I realized that on that particular afternoon, I would find no answers to my questions. I took one step closer and said, "Take care of yourself." I thought about touching her arm, but I had been warned by a nurse that touch might not be welcome, so I repeated, "Take care, Irene," then turned, wove my way through the other pastel-robed statues, and walked out of the room.

During my streetcar ride home, I swore that for my next visit, I would ask Freddie to wait for me in the car—even if I felt too sad or too numb to participate in a sensible conversation.

I paid my sister two more visits before the hospital said that Dad or Mama could visit—one or the other but not both at the same time. It was Dad I decided to ask, and Mama didn't seem to mind. I asked Freddie if he would drive us and, of course, he said he would.

On the thirty-minute drive to the hospital, Dad cleared his throat every thirty seconds, drummed his fingers against the back seat car window, and, although he didn't light a cigarette, reached for one at least twenty times.

As soon as Freddie let us off at the entrance, I took my father's arm. Although Dad had always seemed unemotional in matters relating to his children, and, certainly, I'd never seen him cry, I knew he'd been touched by the life of his youngest child. What I used to tell myself was a "dreamy" look in his eyes, I now felt was a sadness that went far back into some personal darkness that I would never know. I wanted to protect him. It was as simple as that.

An attendant walked us into the visiting room–solarium where, again, Irene stood alone facing a window—standing but certainly not looking out. Twice I said "Hello, Irene." Each time, she nodded without turning, and I realized she'd recently been given extra sedation.

I stepped closer and tapped her shoulder. "Dad's here, Irene." When she didn't turn, I turned back to my father and held up a finger to signal "wait a minute." Then I turned back to Irene, stepped closer, and lightly touched her arm. *Please acknowledge him*—I whispered to myself—*please let him know you know he's here.*

She turned three-quarters of the way toward our father, turning like a mannequin in a department store window, but at least she turned.

Dad dropped his head in a silent nod of greeting. His lips moved but if he spoke, I never heard the words. He stood and waited.

I waited.

Irene waited.

I waited again.

After what seemed like a year, "Hello Dad" emerged from between my sister's lips. Then, as quickly as the words were spoken, my sister turned away.

After my visits to the hospital, Mama said very little. Whether she spoke to Dad after he came with us, I will never know.

Mary Ellen stopped me regularly to ask how Irene was doing. I would answer, "better," or "coming along"—even though neither answer was true, and though Edna must have talked regularly with Mary Ellen about Irene, she called weekly to ask how Irene was.

"Okay, I suppose," I would answer—or "they say she's doing all right." Eventually I got closer to the truth and said, "Irene doesn't say much, so it's really hard to tell."

In late February, I received a call from Anthony's mother, whom I'd known since I was little girl. She wanted to know what to tell Anthony about Irene. He was having nightmares about monsters kidnapping people and kept asking his mother, "Where is Irene?"

"What can I tell him? I don't know what to say, and he seems to know whatever I say isn't the truth. I certainly can't tell him Irene cut herself with a knife and that they put her in a . . . well . . . a . . ."

"You mean in a place for crazy people? Is that what you can't tell him?"

"Now, Lottie, I wouldn't ever say something like that!"

I wanted to say "no but you'd think it, wouldn't you?" but I took in a huge breath and said, "Sorry. I get upset easily on the subject of what people say about my sister. Tell him you talked to me and that I'll pay him a visit to tell him more about how she is."

"You won't . . . I mean . . ."

"Tell him the truth? Of course not!" I started to add—why should I break a family tradition and talk about the way things really are? Instead, I said, "Give me a couple of weeks and I'll stop by and see Anthony when he's at Usma's one afternoon."

I wasn't sure what I was going to say to Anthony, but I knew he needed something closer to the truth than anything his mother or grandmother would come up with. Anthony was much too smart and too sensitive to lie to about someone who had become a good friend.

As luck would have it, two weeks after the phone call from Anthony's mother, I was in Sugar's Drugstore one Saturday when Anthony was there with his grandmother. I waited until Soutine was busy at the pharmacy counter and Anthony was looking at candy in the center aisle.

I walked up to him and gently but quickly told him his mother had mentioned to me that he wanted to know what had happened to Irene. I told him that Irene hadn't been feeling well and had gone away to a place where they were helping her feel better. "I know you're concerned about your cousin, but I promise you, she's fine."

He thought about this then added, "Do you see her?"

I nodded.

"Well, then, tell her I said 'Hi.' "

Then he called out as I started down the aisle. "And be sure to tell her it's 'hi' from Anthony and that I'm doing well in school."

.   .   .

At the beginning of March, after three months of what was reported as "very little improvement," a hospital administrator called me, as the family spokesperson, to ask if electric shock therapy was something I would allow. Anesthesia would be administered, which made the treatment something the family had to approve.

I went to the library and read up on the therapy. The procedure sounded bizarre and even cruel, but I was assured that my sister would be asleep during the procedure—that she might have a headache afterwards but that otherwise, she wouldn't have any idea that a "procedure" had taken place. The treatment had been widely practiced in Europe and was being used in the better mental hospitals in the United States.

I reported on what I read to Freddie. He listened but had little to say. During the weeks it took me to decide, I never felt so entirely alone. Eventually, I agreed.

That year, March blew in like a hundred lions. Even though the shock treatments were to begin one week into that month, my main concern was that inside that cavernous building, my sister would manage to stay warm. At the end of the month, the hospital reported that the therapy seemed to be lifting her depressive mood. Two weeks later, the hospital told me I was welcome to visit.

On the first day I saw her after the shock treatments, I actually carried on a conversation with Irene, even though Irene's memory of why she was in the hospital, of Mama's marriage plans for her, even of Ralph Alan's being married seemed to have been erased. She managed to ask reasonable questions and to give appropriate answers to mine, as long as I didn't touch on any part of her most recent past.

On my second visit, on a sunny day near the end of April, Irene walked with me onto the grounds. When she leaned down to touch the petals of a tulip and said, "Soft, Lottie. They're so unbelievably soft," I felt my first real hope that my sister might be recovering and one day would come home.

Instead of arranging for Mama to see Irene at St. Elizabeth's, I told her it seemed likely that within weeks, Irene would be given a pass for a weekend visit home. That afternoon, Mama began chopping dates and grinding nuts for the baked sweets my sister liked so much. When I reminded Mama that it would be at least a month before Irene actually could visit, she seemed disappointed, although two days later she was chopping and grinding and cooking again. The day before my next visit to the hospital,

Mama presented me with a blue-and-white cookie tin full of Irene's favorite cakes and said, "You take."

Eventually, my sister was issued a weekend pass for the last weekend in May. Every day the week before Irene's visit, Mama asked, "Irene okay now?" And on the day we were to bring her home, Mama seemed to end every sentence with, "What time she come?" During that week, Mama had made enough stuffed squash and *kibbeh* to feed an army.

For that weekend, Mama stayed mainly in the kitchen. Irene spent most of her time in her room. I made a point of letting my sister have the quiet she needed and tried not to worry about what she was doing during the long, silent hours behind the closed door of her room. Dad, too, kept his distance, but at dinner, he glanced regularly toward his youngest daughter with the faintest of smiles.

On Irene's second night at home, I knocked on her bedroom door. "Don't bother to open it, Irene. I just wanted to say it's good to have you home."

As I turned away, I heard her door open. "Thank you, Lottie. Through all of this, you've been so good." Immediately, the door clicked closed.

My sister came home twice during the month of June, and for two weekends during July, she was allowed to visit for three full days. Although she continued to spend hours in her room, she also began to help Mama in the kitchen. She seemed to enjoy shelling peas and snapping beans, helping Mama grind dates or lamb, repetitive tasks that required little thought. She even took up the embroidery Mama had tried to teach her last year, bending her head over the tiny stitches, squinting as she chose the right colored thread.

I worried that she never hummed and never tried to sing. I stayed away from topics that might remind me how much her memory might have been impaired. Over and over again, I told myself, "this will take time."

.   .   .

One evening after dinner, when Irene had retreated to her room, Mama shuffled into the kitchen, where I was finishing my coffee. She wiped her hands on her apron and sat down. She stared at the far edge of the table until, finally, she spoke. "You tink—you tink maybe if Irene hab good Syrian husband, she be okay?"

I didn't know whether to laugh or to scream. I took another sip of coffee and laid down my cup slowly enough to regain my composure. "Mama, listen to me. If Soutine or any of the other ladies has been talking to you about finding Irene a husband, forget it—absolutely forget it. Promise me you will."

She looked at me with puzzled eyes.

"Mama, Irene is not like the Syrian girls at the church! She's different—that's what makes her special. Marrying isn't something she wants to do right now. Promise me you won't mention marrying to Irene." I waited then said again, "Promise me, please!"

Eventually, she nodded.

"Irene is going through difficult feelings right now that are causing her a lot of pain."

Mama shook her head. "No unnerstan."

"I know you don't understand. Just remember what I said. When the ladies talk to you, remember they don't understand either. And do not ever bring up the idea of marrying to Irene. Do you understand what I'm saying?"

Looking as if she'd just been punished, Mama was quiet for a moment, eventually nodded, then stood up, took off her apron, and left the room.

Soon after Irene began coming home, Anthony's mother called to ask if Anthony could possibly see Irene. We agreed that Freddie and I would take Irene and Anthony for a drive into Virginia for ice cream one July afternoon.

Although she was quiet for most of the ride, Irene seemed glad to see Anthony, who'd been warned that Irene was tired and "not quite herself."

Ice cream made the afternoon worthwhile for Anthony, who scraped every last trace of vanilla and chocolate fudge from the bottom of his dish. He laughed at Freddie's riddles and silly jokes. Although Irene was quiet, Anthony glanced regularly in her direction and smiled.

On the ride home, Irene managed to ask Anthony how his year at school had been, and he launched into a detailed explanation about long division and "dividing with two numbers." When he asked Irene if she'd had trouble with arithmetic in school, my sister said, "I don't remember too well, Anthony, but you can do it. You can do a lot of things."

For Anthony, that statement seemed to make the afternoon worthwhile, and when we dropped him off at his grandmother's house, I heard him say, "You be sure to get better now, Irene. Then we can play 'go fish' and maybe even visit Glen Echo again."

In the middle of washing dishes that night, Irene turned to me, "Anthony's very special. He deserves to be able to see his father one day, and I hope that's something that happens soon."

As soon as Irene came home for her first visit, Mary Ellen called to see if she and Edna could stop by just to say "hello" or whether Irene could possibly go over there for cookies and tea.

I waited several weeks before telling Irene that Mary Ellen had called. "They miss you a lot. While you were in the hospital, they called here regularly to see how you were."

Irene seemed puzzled then said, "Baltimore. Didn't they want me to go to Baltimore?"

The question threw me until I remembered that the two women had talked about arranging a scholarship for Irene to attend a summer music program at the Peabody Institute of Music.

"Yes, there was mention of something like that, but right now, they just want to see you. They like you, and they miss you."

Irene was quiet for a moment. "I don't think so, Lottie—I can't really go away from home while I have so many things to do. Besides, Mama will miss me. No—please tell them 'no.' "

The next night, after Freddie drove me home from work, he turned off the car engine and turned toward me. "What's the matter, Lottie? Something really upset you, hasn't it?"

I told him about the conversation I'd had with Irene about Mary Ellen and Edna, then I flopped into his arms and cried and cried. I felt as if Freddie had stuck a pin into the balloon of worry and sadness that seemed to be who I was during those days. I babbled on about feeling exhausted, about being wrung out from protecting Irene and explaining things to Mama with the desperate hope that she would understand.

Freddie held me and stroked my hair and didn't try to reason or talk me out of what I was feeling.

"I keep asking myself—how can I marry and have children. How can I even think about it while my sister doesn't have a life at all?"

"She doesn't have a life right now because she's been sick, kind of like having your leg in a cast or being on a diet of special pills. The doctors are helping her, Lottie, you know that, but she's not going to get better in one day"

"How do you know she will get better?"

"How you know that she won't? Maybe she'll start singing again—not today or tomorrow. She's still young—very young. Maybe she'll meet someone . . . you never . . ."

I laid my finger on his lips. "Just hold me. Hold me and make all this go away."

He was silent for a moment, then kissed the top of my head. "I wish I could make it go away. I really wish I could."

When, finally, I felt ready to walk up the stairs into Mama's house, Freddie, as always, walked me to the door.

On the porch, he took my hands. "Let's not wait too long to get married, Lottie. Irene's life, however it turns out to be, is going to go its own way, and there's only so much worrying you can do. But for us . . ."

"You mean, you and I are getting older and you'd prefer to marry me before every hair on my head turns gray?"

He kissed me lightly. "I think tomorrow morning would be the best time for us to marry, but since that's not likely to happen, please think about December. Think about marrying me before the end of the year."

As July melted into August, Irene seemed to improve—or at least there were no major setbacks. When she was at home, she talked to me about being in the hospital and about the past two years. She'd had two more shock treatments between the end of June and the end of July, and by mid-August she seemed to have adjusted to going and coming between St. Elizabeth's and home.

Shortly before she was to return to the hospital on a hot August afternoon, Dad walked into the kitchen with his long fingers wrapped around something in the palm of his hand.

Irene told me that as soon as she saw its chipped green corner edged in tarnished gold, she recognized the icon of a saint Dad had brought with him from Syria over fifty years ago. Though the paint had faded and peeled in places, the icon of a saint with his hand raised in a blessing was the one that had rested against the mirror of Dad's bureau for as long as I could remember.

It was one of the many puzzles about my father—why would a man who never walked inside the Syrian Church and who scoffed at any kind of talk about religion place this icon in a central position on his bureau where he saw it every day?

Irene said he hesitated, then slid his feet forward and held out his hand to her. "You take. Help you get better. Help you come home." He never looked directly into her eyes.

By the end of August, the doctors were talking about an early fall release.

Trying to be casual about it, I talked to Irene about what she might do once she was living at home. I tried not to worry about the fact that, clearly, she had no plan.

I suggested returning to piano lessons and practicing on Mary Ellen's piano next door. I reminded her that she could take courses in order to get her diploma. I suggested that she could work at a music store. Every time I offered a suggestion, my sister would look away. It was all I could do to keep from saying, "Then what on earth will you do? Shell peas and chop dates and nuts with Mama for the rest of your life?"—until I admitted to myself that was exactly what she might have to do.

The thought of Irene's gorgeous voice and exceptional talent being dumped down the drain made me want to scream and cry, but at the end of our conversations about her future, my sister would reach over and pat my hand. "Don't worry, Lottie. I'll find something to do. Really, I'm going to be fine."

Mrs. Yanchus had told me that Ralph Alan's wife had given birth to a baby girl, but I never mentioned it to Irene. All I could think of was that another life was moving forward while Irene's was standing still. I avoided even thinking about the subject and, before long, I'd managed to erase it from my mind.

The last Sunday in August, Dad had gone for his Sunday walk. Mama was down the street with the cousins, and I was enjoying an afternoon with Freddie. Irene sat alone on the front porch.

Ralph Alan came up Prospect Street, pushing his baby daughter in a carriage. He looked up when he passed Mama's house, noticed Irene, waved, and yelled out his familiar, "Hi ya!" Then he picked up his baby and started to climb the stairs.

Later, he told his mother that the moment Irene saw him with the baby, her eyes widened and she sat still as a statue. He yelled to her again, expecting her to start down the stairs to meet him, to smile and run down the stairs to see the baby. When she continued to be immobilized, Ralph Alan stopped climbing the stairs. My sister stood up, turned "like she was walking in her sleep," and ran into the house and slammed the door.

It was a phone call from Mrs. Yanchus that alerted Dad to what had happened. He walked into Irene's room and found her sprawled across her bed. She looked up at him with tears streaming down her face and pleaded, "Take me back there, please! Oh, please Dad, have them take me back!"

Two sets of shock treatments were given one week apart. The doctor contacted me and said Irene seemed able to remember the incident about Ralph Alan and his baby, and although she didn't want to talk about it, she assured the doctor that she was going to be all right.

For the rest of September, the reports from the hospital were good, and the possibility of a final release was talked about for the first week in November. Once I started visiting my sister again, I was inclined to agree that she might be ready to leave. We talked about her working toward her high school diploma, and I felt better about the idea of her coming home.

As her release date came closer, whenever I began to worry, Freddie assured me that the hospital was an excellent one and that the doctors wouldn't release her if they still had major concerns. He reminded me that setbacks would occur but that it was time for all of us to move on. Two weeks before her release, Irene agreed to drive to Hains Point with Freddie and me. We walked and bought ice cream. Irene even started to hum as we were driving home.

That evening, I told her that Freddie had arranged phone conversations between Anthony's mother and his father and that, with Freddie's help, a train trip was being planned so that Anthony could see his father for the first time in almost five years.

Irene said, "Freddie's really a wonderful person, isn't he?" That's when I decided to tell her that Freddie and I were planning to marry before the end of the year.

My sister covered my hand with hers. "I'm glad, Lottie. Freddie's sweet. He really is."

"We decided not to wait much longer because, well, I want to have plenty of time to make a baby before I get too old." I looked at my sister for signs of sadness about the fact that this hadn't been in the cards for her so far.

Irene smiled. "That certainly will make Mama happy, won't it? A grandchild from you, possibly two."

I laughed. "I can hear her telling any of the Syrian Ladies' Club members who make the mistake of listening, 'Lottie make baby. Maybe Lottie make two!'"

At that point, I specifically recall that my sister and I had leaned in toward each other and laughed.

Two days before she was scheduled to be released from the hospital, Irene went with a group from the hospital to visit the zoo. The November day was warm. Chrysanthemums and lingering roses bloomed, and the sun shone on leafy treasures of reds, oranges, yellows, and greens.

At two-thirty, fifteen minutes before Irene's group was to be called together to board the bus, my sister slipped through the zoo's side gate and started down Connecticut Avenue toward the Calvert Street Bridge.

At ten after three, my sister stepped onto the bridge and began her walk to its center. I like to think Irene's step was lively, her face relaxed and calm.

Unlike today, few cars sped along Rock Creek Parkway twenty-five feet below. The bridge was lined on each side with oak and locust and poplar trees reaching their arms toward the cloudless sky. The spaces between were filled with the shiny leaves of laurel and the darker accent of scrub pine. Below the bridge lay a thin ribbon of highway and the curve of Rock Creek as it wound its way toward the Potomac.

Later, a policeman told us that Irene had walked slowly across the bridge like someone out on an afternoon stroll, that her coat was unbuttoned, that the folds of her dress billowed out and back with the breeze, and that twice she raised her hand to smooth back her hair. When she stopped close to the center of the bridge and leaned over the precipice to look down, the officer assumed she was taking in the fall colors of the scene below. When she put one foot up, using one hand to grasp the cement pillar for support then pushed herself up onto the railing to stand, he was stunned by the swiftness of her move.

"You'll just hold out your arms and feel the air," Ralph Alan had said when she had asked him how to swim toward the light.

I need to think there was hope in my sister's heart as she raised her face toward the sky and that her arms spread wide in a gesture that embraced the heavens because she believed that there she would finally find peace.

The policeman said that one arm went into the air. Then the other arm let go. She balanced. One foot reached, then the other. It was as if, the policeman said, she tried to walk into the air.

"Like a glass broken in a thousand pieces," the ambulance driver told me later. "Pavement, you know. It hardly mattered that there weren't so many cars."

It seemed fitting that the men who carried my sister's coffin said her casket seemed light—amazingly light.